STRIKING DISTANCE

LOVE UNDERCOVER, BOOK 2

LK SHAW

Want a **FREE** short story?
What about **FREE** chapters of **FOREVER** delivered to your inbox?

Be sure to sign up for my newsletter and download your copy of A Birthday Spanking, a Doms of Club Eden prequel! You'll also start receiving bi-weekly chapters of the novella Forever

You'll also receive infrequent updates about what I'm working on, alerts for sales and new releases, and other stuff I don't share elsewhere!

❀ Created with Vellum

Doms of Club Eden

Submission

Desire

Redemption

Protect

Betrayal

My Christmas Dom

Absolution

Forever (A prequel) - Coming July 2020

Love Undercover Series

In Too Deep

Striking Distance

Atonement

Other Books

Love Notes: A Dark Romance

SEALs in Love

Say Yes

Black Light: Possession

Saving Evie: A Brotherhood Protectors

CHAPTER 1

FAINT SHADOWS WERE CAST across the pavement as I hoofed it across the nearly deserted parking lot, tugging my messenger bag full of graded papers against my hip. The closer I got to my car, the faster my steps grew, and a trickle of uneasiness settled over me. The air thickened with a heavy tension that threatened to choke me. Even the normally chirping critters who came out at dusk were quiet and still. I scanned my surroundings, but there were only a few cars scattered here and there.

Cursing myself for overreacting, I slowed my steps and ignored the lead weight in my belly. I reached my car and tossed my bag across the inside of the vehicle to land with a thud on the passenger seat.

A warm, strong hand clapped over my mouth. My scream was muffled behind the tight grip. I scratched and clawed at the other hand that wrapped around my waist pulling me away from the safety of my car. The strong scent of expensive cologne hit my nose, and heavily accented words pierced my eardrums despite my struggles and strangled cries for help. "You may not be that *puta*, but you'll lead me to her."

My heels dragged along the pavement. My chest burned with the need to pull in air. My brain screamed at me to think. A surge of adrenaline kicked in, and I called on all the self-defense techniques Ines had taught me. I fought back, slamming my head backward as hard as I could. The crunch of my skull connecting with the face behind me sounded loud in my ears, but I didn't have time to savor it.

"*Mierda!*" The curse came out nasally.

My body went totally limp, and I slid out of his grip, dropping to my knees. I quickly rammed my elbow up and into the groin of my assailant. Ignoring his bellow of pain, I jumped to my feet and ran as fast as I could back to the school, my ragged breaths echoing through the cool evening air.

I raced down the hallways, hollering. "Somebody, help!"

I collided with a soft body, and my scream was piercing.

"Ms. Jenkins, what's wrong?"

I pulled back at Willie's voice. "Call 9-1-1 now. Someone just tried to grab me in the parking lot."

"Shit. Come on." He tugged me into the nearby janitor closet and locked the door behind us. I wrapped my arms around myself to try and control my shivering while he pulled a cell phone out of his pocket. "Are you okay?"

I absently nodded, my entire focus on the door, and prayed the unknown man didn't try and enter. I only vaguely heard Willie talking next to me.

"The police are on their way."

I blinked and locked eyes with him still holding the phone to his ear. At his words, my adrenaline high crashed, and I burst into tears. He wrapped an arm around me, and I cried against his shoulder. My tears eventually stopped. Pounding footsteps and loud voices interrupted the silence. "Secure the area. Check every nearby room."

We waited. Finally we heard a chorus of "All clear."

A loud knock on the door made me jump.

"Police, is everyone all right?"

Willie opened the door, keeping me behind him. I spotted the first uniformed officer over his shoulder, and my body sagged in relief. My eyes moved to the second man, and my heart skipped a beat, then started another wild pulsing in my chest. *Victor*.

The first officer shifted, blocking my view, and our connection was severed. "Miss? Is everyone okay?"

"Yes," I focused on his words. "Sorry."

"I'm Officer Gladstone and this is my partner, Officer Rodriguez. Can you tell me your name?"

"Estelle Jenkins."

"Miss Jenkins, why don't we step in here and you can tell us what happened?"

He gestured to the nearest classroom and pulled out a notepad.

"Do you need me for anything?" Willie asked.

The two officers exchanged glances and Gladstone shook his head. "Not at the moment, but we may call you in to answer some questions."

"I'll be here a little while longer. Come find me. I'm glad you're okay Ms. Jenkins."

"Thank you for your help, Willie." I hugged him before he disappeared down the hall.

I led us inside while Gladstone called into dispatch, acutely aware of Victor on my heels.

"Our forensics team is on the way. Now, I understand

someone grabbed you in the parking lot. Can you tell me anything about your assailant? Man or woman? Height? Hair color? Any details you can recall would be extremely helpful, no matter how small you think it might be."

"It all happened so fast. Definitely a man. He came up from behind me, so I didn't get a look at him. Once I got free, I just ran."

"Do you mind if I ask how you escaped?" He paused in his writing.

"I dropped to my knees and shoved my elbow straight into his nuts. Then I took off running."

Both men winced and shifted uncomfortably.

"Oh, there is one thing. He spoke with a heavy Spanish accent. Called me a *puta*. Said something about me not being her, but I can't recall his exact words. I'm sorry."

Finally, Victor spoke. "It could have been Miguel Álvarez."

I sucked in a breath. My gaze darted to meet his. "After all this time? Why now? And how would he even know about me? I never met him personally. Only Alejandro, and he's dead."

Victor scoffed. "The D.E.A. has been looking for Álvarez since he escaped, but rumor has it he's been spending these last months doing everything he can to rebuild his empire. He still has loyal employees. Ones who no doubt saw you with Ines. She never should have stayed in contact with you while she was undercover. He knows he can use you to get to her."

He paced, running one hand through his hair, and it was then I finally noticed how tense he was. His jaw was clenched, and I'd never seen that expression on his face before. It was filled with so much rage. His brown eyes were as dark as pitch, and his fists were balled at his sides.

A throat cleared and we both glanced over at the other officer I'd forgotten was in the room. His gaze darted between the two of us. "Does someone want to fill me in on what you two are talking about? It's obvious you know each other, and have intel I don't."

"It's possible our perp is Miguel Álvarez."

Gladstone's eyes bulged. "As in the head of the Juárez Cartel? Why the fuck would he want to kidnap Miss Jenkins?" He darted an abashed glance in my direction. "Pardon the language, ma'am."

I waved him off. It wasn't like I hadn't heard the word before. I was practically raised in the Rodriguez household. One made entirely of boys, aside from Ines.

Victor gave his partner a brief rundown. "It was kept quiet, but about eight months ago, my sister went undercover to find our missing brother. When it was all said and done, Álvarez escaped, and his nephew, Alejandro, was dead. His entire empire was taken down by an undercover D.E.A. agent. My guess is he wants revenge against my sister and Brody. Estelle is the key to that."

"No way. I'm not the key to anything. I don't know anything of value to him. I don't even know exactly where Ines and Brody are. They said it was safer that way."

"It's possible Álvarez thinks otherwise."

The door opened. Both men went for their weapons at the same time. Victor pulled me behind him. A man wearing a forensics shirt stepped into the room, and everyone relaxed. Guns were put away.

"We're still processing the scene, but we found this on the

ground outside the vehicle." He held out my messenger bag. "We didn't bother dusting it for fingerprints due to the fabric. You might want to check and make sure everything's there."

Victor took the bag from his hand and gave it to me. I was careful not to touch him.

"My cell phone and wallet are gone."

He cursed. "He has your ID. He knows where you live."

My stomach sank. "What does that mean?"

Officer Gladstone answered. "It means you go home and hope this was a random incident."

"And if it wasn't?"

He put his notepad back in his pocket. "If you're uncomfortable with that idea, we can request a patrol car to periodically stop by and check on you. A more drastic option, and more difficult one to get approved, is you can request to stay in a safe house."

"Or you can stay with us," Victor added.

My eyes darted over to meet his, and I was already shaking my head. No way was I staying at the Rodriguez house. Not with Victor there. I'd take my chances requesting either a patrol car or a safe house.

I turned to Gladstone. "If a safe house was approved, what all would that entail?"

CHAPTER 2

"IF THE REQUEST WAS GRANTED, it would mean you'd stay in a safe house 24/7, with round the clock protection until we are able to identify the suspect and apprehend him. No one would know the location except the officers assigned to guard you and our Captain," Gladstone explained.

Estelle blinked and reared back. "What do you mean 24/7? What about my job? I have to come to work. And if you don't ever identify him? I can't stay there indefinitely. What if this is all just a mistake, and I wasn't the intended victim? Or it was a random incident? No, I can't do that."

I butted in. "Which is why I suggested you come stay at our house. You'd have protection but could still come to work. One of us would bring you here and pick you up. At least until the perp is flushed out and taken into custody."

I wasn't sure why I was pushing for her to stay with my father, brother, and me. When the call came across the radio about a possible attempted kidnapping at Rivers Elementary, I never expected it to be Estelle. At the sight of her blue eyes, red-rimmed and full of fear, my blood had chilled in my veins.

Estelle glared at me. "You don't even know that it's really me he was after."

I threw my hands up. "God, you're frustrating."

"Let's all take a deep breath here," my partner intervened. "Miss Jenkins, I understand about wanting to keep your schedule as regular as possible, but you also need to think about your safety. Someone just attempted to abduct you. It's possible he could try again."

Estelle fisted her hands at her hips. "I'm well aware of the safety concerns you might have. I also have an obligation to the children in my class. One I don't take lightly. Which is the *only* reason I'm considering staying at the Rodriguez household. I trust that family to protect me."

About time. "I'll put a call in to my father. He'll get Ines' room ready for you."

She didn't meet my eyes for several seconds. Finally, they collided with mine, and I saw the reluctant acceptance in them. "Fine. I'll need to get some of my things from home first."

I turned to my partner. "I'll talk to the Captain and let him know what's going on. We'll need to put out another APB on Álvarez. See if anyone has any info on him. The last intel we had was that he was still hiding out somewhere in Mexico, but even that is a couple months old. The D.E.A. can't seem to find him."

Gladstone shook his head. "I don't think any of this is a good idea."

"She needs protection, and if this is the only way to provide it, then we'll make it work."

"*She* is right here." Estelle sent us a mocking wave and

forced smile. "I'm agreeing to *temporarily* stay, but when you realize that today was just a mistake, I'm going back to my house."

I frowned at her words. I'd forgotten how stubborn she was.

Gladstone, always the peacemaker, reassured her. "I'm sure it is only temporary, and you'll be back home in no time."

Estelle closed her eyes and took a deep breath. She opened them again and let out a huff of air, a few stray strands of hair fluttering above her forehead from the force of it. Her eyes locked on mine. She'd accepted her fate.

"Are you ready, then?"

"I suppose. I'll just follow you over."

I shook my head. "We'll need to make sure forensics is done processing the scene. We may have to come back and get your car tomorrow."

Estelle tightened her lips and her jaw tensed, but she nodded. "Fine. Let's go."

I SLOWLY CREPT up the stairs, careful not to disturb anyone. I'd just finished my shift, and it was late. No sooner did my foot hit the top step than the door to Ines' room opened and Estelle stepped out wearing an oversized sweatshirt with Loyola University printed across the front. My entire focus homed in on her long, smooth legs below the hemline. A hemline she had suddenly tugged down almost to knee length. Estelle hunched over as she tried to cover herself.

"What are you doing creeping around in the hallway?" she snapped.

I raised an eyebrow. "I'm not creeping. I live here. I just got home, and I'm on my way to my room." I pointed past her.

Estelle glanced in that direction, and I could just see her face flush in the light given off by the nightlight my father insisted go in the hallway.

"Why are you walking around the house half naked anyway? What if Pablo had come out of his room?"

"I'm not half naked. Besides, normal people are asleep right now, not skulking around in hallways. And not that it's any of your business, but I was on my way to the bathroom."

I jerked my chin forward. "It's right over there."

Estelle glared daggers at me still trying to keep herself covered. "I know where it is, thank you. Now, if you'd kindly go to your room and close the door."

I laughed. "Good lord, I've seen your bare legs. It's not like it's the first time. You and Ines used to parade around here in bathing suits skimpier than what you're wearing now."

"That may be so, but we were just kids then. We're adults now. I mean, it's not like I want to see you walking around in a Speedo or anything."

"I wouldn't be caught dead in a Speedo."

I walked past her, and just as I reached my room, I turned. "For the record, if you did catch me walking to the bathroom in the middle of the night, all you'd see is me in my birthday suit."

I winked before closing the door on her wide-eyed expression. Chuckling at having the last word, I removed my uniform. I stowed my gun belt safely on top of my dresser and unbuttoned my shirt, my thoughts drifting to Estelle. I'd always considered her another sister. That was, until she turned sixteen. The memory of that day was still so vivid in my head.

I could hear the two of them giggling all the way from the bottom of the stairs. Good god, they were loud, and only getting louder as I took the steps two at a time on the way to my room at the end of the hall. Just as I reached Ines' room, the door opened and a warm, soft body collided with mine.

Instinctively, I grabbed her hips to keep her from tumbling to the ground. My eyes met startled blue ones, and everything froze. It was as though time stood still while Estelle and I stared at each other. When did she become so beautiful?

She smiled shyly, her face a little flushed, but she didn't look away.

"Vicky, you're home!"

Ines' excited scream jolted us back to reality, and my hands jerked away from Estelle like I'd burnt them on a hot stove. I shoved them in my pocket still feeling them tingle. Her expression faltered, but then she turned to smile at Ines like the connection we'd had was nothing. I pushed away the sting of it and forced myself to forget about how, for a brief moment, my world had shifted.

That was a lifetime ago. Now she was here, in my house, for who knew how long. I'd be a single room away from her night after night. No doubt tonight was only the first of many in which we'd run across each other in the darkness. I slid into bed cursing the fact that the one woman I shouldn't be attracted to lay only a few feet away.

CHAPTER 3

WITH A GROAN, I slammed my palm down on the alarm clock, silencing the obnoxious noise. I'd borrowed it from Ernesto last night since I didn't have my cell, and I had to make sure I got up on time for work this morning. I reluctantly crawled out of bed, not quite ready to start my day. It had taken me forever to fall asleep after my encounter with Victor last night. Hoping to avoid a repeat performance, I sent up a quick prayer, grabbed the clothes I'd laid out and my bag of toiletries. I cracked the door open to make sure the coast was clear. Then I hustled into the hallway before disappearing into the bathroom. After a quick shower, I dressed, and went back to my room for my messenger bag. Sounds of life floated through the air as I made my way down the stairs and into the kitchen.

"Good morning, *mi burbujita.*"

I smiled at the familiar nickname of "little bubbles".

"Morning, Ernesto."

Ines' father was like a dad to me. More than my biological one ever had been.

"I made breakfast. Victor should be down soon."

"Thank you, but you didn't need to go to the trouble."

He shooed me over to the table and brought over a plate stacked with several homemade stuffed gorditas. I'd never be able to eat all three of them. No matter how delicious they were.

"I have nothing better to do this morning than to cook for a beautiful woman." He flirted with a wink, one far more charming than his youngest son's.

"Morning, Dad. Estelle." Victor stepped into the kitchen wearing a tight, muscle enhancing white t-shirt and a pair of gray sweatpants that left little to the imagination. Not that I was imagining. I jerked my gaze away.

"Grab a plate, son."

I met Victor's eyes. He smiled smugly. *Crap. Why was I even staring at him anyway?* I shifted my eyes to my food and suddenly found the chorizo, potato, and avocado inside the small corn pocket extremely interesting.

"Pablo tells me they've put out another APB on Álvarez," Ernesto said once he and Victor sat down to eat.

"Yes, sir. I also called Ines yesterday to let her know what happened. Of course she wanted to race back here, but I told her it wasn't safe. She and Brody will stay put for now."

I set down my gordita. "I hate that she isn't here, but I know how important it is that they stay out of Chicago."

"If it *is* the cartel behind the attack yesterday, then the two of them definitely need to keep hiding out."

"Morning everyone," a loud voice called out from near the den. Ines' brother, Manuel, came into view. "Looks like I got here right on time."

He plucked one of the gorditas off Victor's plate.

"Hey, asshole, get your own."

Manuel only laughed. He rustled Victor's hair, who jerked away, before grabbing a plate and stacking it with more small hash pouches.

Ernesto shook his head at his son's antics. "Doesn't Marguerite feed you at home?"

"Of course she does, but I'm a growing boy who's hungry again."

"You're thirty-five. Hardly a child," Victor bit out.

I frowned at his tone. He sounded angry, and his fingers were threaded tightly together on top of the table. What was going on between the two of them?

"Doesn't make me any less hungry." Manuel sat to my left and, after a smiling greeting, dug into his food.

"Here," I offered Victor the remaining gordita on my plate. "I can't eat anymore, and I don't want it to go to waste."

He took it and finished the rest of the meal in silence while Ernesto and Manuel switched topics. Once everyone was done eating, I stood to take my plate to the sink.

Ernesto tutted. "Sit and finish your juice. I'll take care of the dishes."

"That's hardly fair that you have to cook *and* clean. I may be here a while. I can certainly pitch in and help."

He patted me lovingly on the cheek. "Today, you are a guest. You can help another day."

Giving in with a sigh, I handed him my plate and sat back down.

Victor dug into his pocket. "Before I forget, I found an old cell phone you can use until you're able to get a new one."

He handed it to me.

"Thank you."

"I'm going to run upstairs and get my keys, and then I'll take you to work. We can get your car after, and I'll follow you back here."

"Are you not working?"

"Not today."

"We'll set up a schedule, so one of us will always take you to work and pick you up," Ernesto added.

"If I have my own vehicle, why can't I just drive myself?"

"Because hopefully, the police escort will make someone think twice about trying to grab you again," Victor explained.

What he said made sense, but I wasn't keen on relying on anyone. I'd always taken care of myself. I got a job the minute I was old enough to work. Bought my own car. My own house. Never once had I ever asked anyone for help. Having to do so now was like an itch I couldn't scratch. It ate at me. "Fine."

"If there's no other objections, I'll be back in a minute." Victor disappeared out of the room leaving me with Manuel and Ernesto, whose forehead was crinkled and normally smiling lips were turned downward. He glanced in my direction, and shifted back into the oft-smiling man I was used to.

"You don't have to worry about a thing Estelle. Victor will make sure nothing happens to you."

I smiled at the pride in his voice.

"Thank you, Ernesto, I'm sure he will. I guess I better get going. Thank you as well for breakfast." I leaned down to brush a kiss over his cheek, and his familiar woodsy and leather fragrance reminded me of some of the happiest times of my childhood.

I grabbed my bag and headed out to the living room to wait for Victor. Within a moment he was back downstairs.

"You ready?"

I nodded.

Once we were in his truck and on our way, I couldn't hold back my curiosity.

"What was that little exchange back there with Manuel?"

Victor stiffened.

"I'm not sure what you mean."

I stared hard at him, not believing his feigned ignorance. "You were overly annoyed with him. I'd even say pissed off."

"I just don't appreciate being treated like a child," he said after a moment.

I studied him. He was serious. "How did he treat you like a child? He was joking and making fun of his never-ending hunger. Seemed like an ongoing joke between him and your dad."

Victor's grip tightened on the steering wheel. "Never mind. You wouldn't understand."

His body language—from his clenched jaw to his stiff shoulders—screamed the topic was over. He wouldn't even look in my direction.

"Sorry. I didn't know it was a touchy subject." Clearly I'd pushed a button.

Victor didn't acknowledge my apology, just kept his eyes on the road. I sat back and, instead of making conversation, my mind drifted back to all the days, months, years even I'd spent at the Rodriguez house. I'd always envied the family's close relationship.

While we continued driving in a now uncomfortable silence, I sent covert glances in Victor's direction. He seemed to have changed. Become harder. Not just more muscular, although he was definitely that, but something else.

But one fact remained. No matter how much time had passed or how much he'd changed, he still made my belly flutter even if I wished he didn't.

CHAPTER 4

I WAS ANNOYED with myself for even mentioning Manuel. What I'd said was true, though. He still treated me like a kid. Even more so now that Ernesto Jr. was dead.

"I'll walk you inside."

Estelle's hand froze on the door handle, and she sent me a look I had trouble interpreting.

"Thank you, but you don't have to. It's not like anyone is going to try anything in broad daylight."

"Maybe. Maybe not. I'd rather play it safe."

She remained silent for another moment and then shrugged. "Suit yourself."

I stayed close to her and could see the caution in each step she took. Like me, her concentration was focused on our surroundings, searching for any disturbance in the air. My gaze darted back and forth across the parking lot, and my whole body was alert for anything out of the ordinary. Anything that seemed out of place. I didn't relax my guard until we stepped inside. I stayed right on her heels as we

23

entered her classroom. Miniature sized desks were lined up perfectly in rows, and bright, happy wall decorations almost hurt my eyes.

"Wow, it's really...colorful in here."

"What did you expect?" She laughed. "It's a room full of six year olds. They chose a lot of the decorations."

Estelle deposited her bag on her desk. I observed her as she walked around straightening chairs and desks that were already straight and organized.

"I guess it's been a while since I've been in a classroom."

"Ten years isn't that long ago."

"It feels like forever. So much has happened since then."

"True. I never imagined we'd be here. Who would have thought, a year ago, that Ines would be in hiding with her lover because the Mexican cartel is after her, and I might need protection from them as well?"

I shuddered. "Don't ever use the words Ines and lover in a sentence together again."

Estelle's expression shifted into mirth. "Really? You're weirded out by Ines and her lover?"

"You can be really aggravating sometimes. You know that, Bubbles?"

Her whole face lit up, and her eyes sparkled with laughter. My gut clenched at the sight.

"You're such a baby. Ines is twenty-six years old. She lost her virginity a long time ago."

Cringing, I plugged my ears with my fingers. "Jesus, that's my sister. I don't want to know anything about what she might be doing."

Estelle rolled her eyes and started writing on the chalkboard. I glanced around once more and then looked out her classroom windows to observe the grounds. No suspicious shadows moved. No random vehicles that seemed out of place. All appeared as it should. The shrill noise of the school bell blasted through the air. My muscles twitched. The sound of feet running through the halls grew louder. The door to the classroom jerked open. I spun to witness several tiny humans enter.

"Good morning, Miss Jenkins," several kids called out at once.

A complete change came over Estelle. A huge smile graced her face, and she appeared completely relaxed and happier than I could ever remember seeing her.

"Good morning."

A light shone from her eyes as she watched them shrug out of their jackets and hang up their backpacks in small cubbies with their name's written above each one. Slowly more students began filing in. Several students paused when they saw me, but otherwise ignored my presence. I felt a tug on my hand, and I glanced down to see the most adorable blonde-haired, blued-eyed girl staring up me.

"Whath *your* name?" she asked, her tongue peeking out between the space where her two front teeth were missing.

"Victor. What's yours?"

"Thadie."

"That's a pretty name."

Like a coquette in training she smiled and played with her hair.

"Thank you. Are you a dad?"

"No, I'm not a dad."

Her face fell. "Oh, cuth I'm looking for a dad, and you look like you'd be a nithe one."

25

"Sadie, honey, we talked about this, remember?" Estelle's gentle voice interrupted us. "You can't keep asking people that."

"I'm thorry Mith Jenkins."

Estelle tugged the little girl to her side. "It's okay sweetie. Why don't you go take a seat? Class will be starting soon."

"Yeth, ma'am."

Sadie moved away and sat down. Soon she was chattering away with the other kids at her table, apparently forgetting the conversation already.

"Well, that was interesting."

"Sorry about that. Her dad ran off a few years ago and she's fixated on finding a new one."

"That sucks. She's a sweet kid."

Estelle's eyes remained on her classroom. "They all are. I love each and every one of my students."

I really studied her and saw the pride in her eyes. She had this glow in their presence. I'd never seen that before. Did she glow like that for her boyfriend as well? She never talked about anyone. *Wait. Why did I even care?*

It didn't matter one way or another to me. I was merely a temporary fixture in her life until Álvarez was either locked away or killed. Personally, I preferred the latter considering the hell he'd put my sister through.

In the meantime, I'd protect Estelle with my life because she was Ines' best friend. I ignored that tiny voice that called me a liar.

SHORTLY AFTER THE last student had arrived, I'd taken a final pass around the building and walked through the parking lot. I didn't notice any new vehicles or anything that set off my internal alarms. Now I was parked next to Estelle's car waiting for her to come out. The door of the school opened, and I straightened from my semi relaxed position against my truck. She spotted me and waved. My heart picked up a beat. Keeping my eyes peeled, I met her partway.

"How was your day? Any meltdowns?"

"Only a minor one at lunch when someone didn't want ketchup on their hamburger. How about you?"

"Mostly a quiet day. Dad and I made a few phones calls to some of our contacts, but their intel came up as empty as ours. No one's been able to locate Álvarez. It could be months, years even, until the D.E.A. find him."

"Months? Years?" Estelle choked out, her mouth hanging open.

"There's a reason Miguel Álvarez was never charged with any crimes. The man is smart. He also knows how to stay hidden. At some point, though, his luck is going to run out. When it does, we'll be ready."

"I never expected it could be that long. I can't stay with you guys forever."

I laid my hand on her shoulder and my fingers tingled. "We'll do the best we can, Estelle."

She sighed. "I know. This is just never how I saw my life as being."

We stopped at her car.

"I know, and I'm sorry. Look, I'm going to follow right behind you. Just to make sure you get home okay."

"Okay, thanks. I guess I'll see you when we get to the house."

"Be careful and keep an eye out."

Estelle nodded gravely before disappearing behind the

wheel. Once I was in my truck, she pulled away. I stayed right on her tail. We hadn't made it a few blocks before I noticed a black Mercedes in my rearview mirror. It stayed with us for several miles. Cursing, I snatched up my cell phone and made a call.

CHAPTER 5

Most of my day had been spent thinking about Victor. My concentration had been off. I'd forgotten a spelling test. I'd read the wrong chapter in our book during story time. More than once, a student had to call my name a couple times before I heard him. It had been weird having him in my classroom, my safe space, seeing an almost intimate part of me. I was decidedly uncomfortable, and I wasn't sure why. Actually that wasn't true. It made me feel vulnerable. Exposed. I didn't particularly care for the feeling. I heard an unfamiliar, high pitched ring, and flinched. It was coming from my bag. Scrambling, I dug through it one-handed, trying to keep my eyes on the road. Finally, I found it.

"Hello?"

"It's Victor," his tone was all business. "I need you to listen closely. I want you to take a left on Parson Road up ahead. Then I want you to make the first right and start heading toward the station house on Walton Street. I called my father, and he's heading this direction."

"What's going on?" My voice trembled.

"I don't know if it's anything or not, but I'm not taking any chances. A vehicle has been following us for the last couple miles."

"Oh, god."

"Listen, everything is going to be fine. Just follow my instructions, and stay on the line."

"Okay."

I took the route he'd told me to, making sure I didn't lose him. Nausea swept over me, and my fingers ached from the death grip I maintained on the steering wheel. Still, I tried not to panic. Victor wouldn't let anything happen to me. My eyes constantly darted up to my rear view mirror confirming he was still right behind me.

"You're doing great Estelle. Hang in there, babe."

I unclenched my fingers, wiggled them to try and get the blood flowing, and put them right back on the steering wheel. Victor sighed in relief as I made another turn.

"A patrol car just pulled them over. I think we're in the clear."

"Are you sure?"

"Yeah, go ahead and start heading toward the house."

"All right."

"I'm going to hang up now. I'll see you at the house."

The rest of the drive was nerve wracking. I couldn't wait to get out of the car and into the safety of the Rodriguez house. It took forever, or maybe it just seemed like it, but finally I pulled into the driveway. I slammed the gearshift into park and grabbed my bag, practically jumping out of the vehicle.

"Estelle, stop."

Victor's command penetrated my brain. I was almost running toward the house. My pace slowed, barely, and he caught up to me. The second his hand touched my arm I lost it. I covered my face and sobbed. He wrapped his arms around me, and I buried my face in his chest.

"You're okay. Everything's fine now. Please stop crying. You know I don't handle women's tears well. I break out into hives."

Despite the fact that wetness poured down my face, I barked out laughter at the ridiculousness of Victor's words. I pulled back and craned my neck to peer up at him. He gently rubbed his thumb across my cheek, taking a few stray tears with him. My breath hitched. His eyes remained fixed on mine, and I lost track of time.

"Better?" he whispered.

Slowly I nodded. "I think so."

"Good. Let's go inside then. I'll make you a stiff drink."

"Sounds like a good idea. I could use one."

"Just don't get drunk and try to take advantage of me, will ya?" He smiled down at me.

Another bubble of laughter escaped. He was trying to put me at ease, and I was grateful.

His expression shifted and suddenly became serious. "I like seeing you laugh."

He still held me in his arms. I cleared my throat and quickly stepped back. A flash of emotion flickered in his eyes.

"Thank you for making me feel better. Sorry I freaked out on you."

"Don't worry about it. It's perfectly understandable."

This time, my retreat into the house was much slower. Inside, I turned to Victor.

"I'm going to run upstairs for a minute. I'll be right back."

"That's fine. I'm going to call my dad, and after I get an update, I'll get that drink for you and start dinner."

With a quick glance over my shoulder to see him still watching me, I headed up the stairs. I closed the bathroom door behind me and stood in front of the mirror staring at my reflection. I wasn't cut out for this. It had only been twenty-four hours, and I already wanted my life back. How did Ines do this kind of thing day in and day out?

I grabbed a washcloth, wet it, and pressed it against my face. I hated that I'd broken down in front of Victor. The thought of being vulnerable in front of anyone, but especially him, and twice in one day, reminded me too much of my childhood. The only person who ever saw the true me was Ines, and she was thousands of miles away.

I took a moment longer to feel sorry for myself, and then I dried off my face, straightened my shoulders, and went back downstairs. I walked into the kitchen to see Victor set his phone down.

"That was my dad. He pulled the car over, but it was only some guy on his way home to Harwood Heights."

The knot in my stomach tightened further instead of relaxing at the news. I'd hoped maybe this would all be over already.

"I guess that means I'm stuck here for now." I wasn't happy, but I was going to have to try and make the best of things.

"Hey, we're not so bad. At least I'm not. I can't say the same for the rest of the family."

What was going on with him and his brothers? "Well, I happen to like your family, so I guess there are worse places I could be stuck."

"This is true. Even now, you could be hiding away in one

of those run-down safe houses with a boring, old cop who isn't nearly as handsome as me."

I rolled my eyes. "You're certainly full of yourself."

"What can I say? It's part of my charm." The boyish smile he sent me made my heartbeat speed up.

"Wow, you are definitely an ego-maniac."

"Yet another charming character trait."

I'd never win an argument against him, so I don't even know why I tried.

"Are you done being obnoxious?"

He actually paused like he was thinking about it. "Probably not."

"Well why doesn't your obnoxious self make me that drink you promised."

He bowed. "As my lady wishes."

He grabbed items out of the liquor cabinet. Before long, I was sitting at the table with a seven and seven.

"Where's Pablo? I haven't seen him since I got here."

Victor moved around the kitchen pulling out pots and pans and then items from the fridge. "I know he worked a double today, but he's also been gone a lot. Who knows? We don't talk much."

"Well, I hope I get a chance to catch up with him."

"I'm sure he'll show up eventually."

I changed the topic. "I don't know why you all insist on cooking for me. While I appreciate it, I'm more than capable of cooking for myself. I've been doing it for years."

He sent me a quick glance before returning back to his task. "I have no doubt you're more than able, but when someone else is willing, it's best to just let them take care of you."

My skin prickled. It was a foreign concept, and one I

didn't trust. Time had taught me that the only person I could count on to take care of me was me.

"Well, thanks."

"You're welcome."

We fell into a comfortable silence while I sipped my drink and Victor cooked. It was obvious he knew his way around a kitchen. Silently, I watched him. Usually we were sniping at each other. I'd never seen this side of him, even though I'd known him for almost my entire life. It stirred up feelings. Feelings I didn't trust. Ones I had no desire to explore further. I'd stay here until this all blew over, and then I could get back to my own place with my own things and forget this all ever happened.

CHAPTER 6

I'D ALWAYS ENJOYED COOKING. Mostly because it was the one thing I did better than all my brothers. None of them could even boil water, so I cooked as often as possible. For some reason I also wanted to impress Estelle. The house phone rang as I was about to put the chicken in the cast iron skillet for fajitas.

"Hello?"

"Where's my daughter?" The woman's speech was slurred and angry. "You can't keep her from me."

"Excuse me?"

"Where is she?" The possibly drunk woman demanded.

"I'm sorry, I don't know who you're talking about."

"Estelle, you idiot. I know she's there. She always ran to you people."

Understanding finally dawned. This was Estelle's mom?

"She's right here, Mrs. Jenkins. Would you like to speak with her?" I glanced up to meet Estelle's eyes. She paused mid-drink, and, in an instant, a change come over her. Her expression tightened, and her fingers clenched around the glass she held.

"Of course I want to speak to her. I've been trying to reach her all day."

Estelle walked over and stood stiffly next to me. Up close I noticed other differences about her. Normally twinkling blue eyes were now dull and lifeless. She was completely void of the internal light she always emitted even during our arguments.

"Yes ma'am. Hold on just a second." A wave of protective instinct rushed through me. Who the fuck did this woman think she was dulling the life of this beautiful person beside me?

Almost reluctantly, Estelle took the phone from my hand.

"Hello, Pauline." Even her voice had changed.

I went back to making dinner, but still listened intently to the one-sided conversation.

"My phone was stolen."

"No, I didn't change my number and not give it to you."

There was a short pause between each answer.

"No, I didn't give any new number to George, either."

Pauline? George? She didn't call her parents Mom and Dad?

"You never call me anyway." Each response was more clipped than the last. I could see Estelle retreating further and further inside herself the longer she remained on the phone.

"Now's not a good time."

Another long pause.

"I'm an adult. I don't need to tell you why I'm at the Rodriguez house. No, Ines isn't here. Look, Pauline, I have to go."

She didn't say goodbye before hanging up the phone. Giving up the pretense that I hadn't heard every word she said, I turned and wiped my hands on a dishtowel.

"Everything okay?"

Without responding, she returned to the table, picked up what remained of her drink, and tossed it back. Then she walked to the liquor cabinet and made another, only this one was straight whiskey. From across the room, tension and anger radiated off her. Her jaw was tight, her movements jerky and angry as she almost slammed the bottle down. Estelle put the glass to her lips, threw her head back, and swallowed it in one go. Well then.

She wiped the wetness from her lips and finally met my eyes. "Everything's just fine."

I'd never seen this side of her before, and my blood boiled. How dare her mother make her feel this way. Was this the kind of relationship they had? Was this why she'd practically lived here as a kid?

"Are you sure? Because that conversation didn't sound 'fine'."

"I'll be more blunt then. I don't really want to talk about it."

I inclined my head. "That's fair."

Estelle rinsed her glass out in the sink. "If you'll excuse me, I'm not feeling well. I'm going up to my room to lie down for a bit."

She disappeared out the door leaving me standing there alone. *What the fuck just happened?*

~

ESTELLE STILL HADN'T COME DOWN by the time supper was

37

finished, so I went upstairs and knocked lightly on her door. The bed squeaked, and I heard footsteps on the floor. The door cracked open. Her eyes still hadn't recovered their sparkle.

"Dinner's ready."

"I'm not really hungry."

"You need to eat." There was no way I was going to let her sit up here by herself any longer and wallow.

"I'm just going to hang out in here and work on grading papers."

"You mean stay up here and feel sorry for yourself?"

She bristled, which was the exact reaction I was looking for. I wanted that glow back in Estelle's eyes, and if it meant pushing her buttons and pissing her off, then that's what I'd do.

"Excuse me?"

"You're indulging in a pity party. I don't know what's going on between you and your mom, but is sitting up here and sulking really making things better?"

With each word I spoke I could see the tinder catch fire, and a tiny flame began to grow.

She opened the door fully. "Pity party? Sulking? Is that what you think I'm doing?"

"That's what it looks like to me." I shrugged nonchalantly.

There was now a full-on bonfire roaring in Estelle's eyes.

"You're such a dick, you know that? I don't understand how Ines puts up with you. You have no idea about my life or what's going on."

"You're right, I don't. I only know you had an obviously shitty conversation with your mom."

She scoffed. "I had a shitty *life* with my mom, which is

why I don't talk to her. Honestly, I'm surprised her drunk ass even thought to call here."

"Then don't let her win by getting to you. Come downstairs, eat, and forget all about her. If you clean your plate, I might even have a special dessert for you after." I waggled my eyebrows suggestively.

"God, you're such a guy."

"What?" I asked innocently. "I was talking about chocolate cake. What did you think I was talking about?"

Estelle shook her head. "Fine. Give me a minute, and I'll be down."

"Hurry up before it gets any colder. My culinary masterpieces deserve to be treated with respect."

I went downstairs and let her do whatever she needed. I was just glad I'd gotten a reaction out of her. It had killed me seeing her look so defeated. A few minutes later I heard her coming. With just a glance, I knew she wasn't back to her normal self, but she was better than when she'd left the room earlier.

"Have a seat. Everything's on the table, so help yourself. I'm just going to grab a bottle of wine."

"Thanks."

We had a quiet but enjoyable meal. An idea came to me, and I laid my fork down. "I have an extra burner phone upstairs. Why don't you give Ines a call? I think it will put her mind at ease hearing your voice. She's worried about you."

"Are you sure? I know it's not safe to talk to her often."

"It'll be fine. I mean you guys can't chat until two a.m. like you used to when you were teenagers, but a ten- or fifteen-minute conversation isn't going to hurt anything."

Estelle's face softened. "Thank you. That means a lot."

"You're welcome. Let me grab it and get her on the line for you. Feel free to use the den, so you can have some privacy."

I went to grab the phone from my dresser drawer. I dialed the number and headed to meet Estelle.

"Hello?"

"Hey, it's me."

"Is Estelle all right?" There was fear in her tone.

"She's fine. She just had a bad day today, and I really think she needs to talk to you."

"What happened?"

"She'll tell you."

I walked into the den. Estelle had her arms wrapped around herself and was staring out the window. She turned at my approach.

"Here she is. I'll let you guys talk for a bit."

I gave her the phone. "I'm going to clean up the kitchen. Try to keep it no longer than fifteen minutes."

"Thank you for doing this for me." Her eyes met mine and their gorgeous blue depths sparkled with happiness again.

"You're welcome."

I left her alone, pleased that I'd been able to bring a smile back to her face.

CHAPTER 7

"Hey, Bubbles."

"Hey, Bunny."

"I've missed you." I plopped onto the recliner and curled my feet underneath me.

"I missed you too."

"You know, I think this is the longest we've ever gone without talking to each other. It really sucks, by the way," I added forlornly.

"Totally sucks. What happened today? Victor told me it was rough."

I harrumphed. "You mean besides the fact that I was almost kidnapped yesterday? Or that I had a breakdown after work when I thought we were being followed? Then, to top off the current shit show that is my life, a drunk Pauline calls your house tonight, and I had to deal with her. In front of your brother, no less. You mean besides that?"

It wasn't fair to be so short and shitty with Ines, but everything was starting to smother me. The minute Victor said my mother was on the phone, my head had started throbbing. It still ached a little.

"Jesus, Estelle, I'm so sorry. I wish I could be there to help you deal with all this. I'm sure the added stress of your mom calling isn't helping the situation. What did she want?"

"The usual. Reminding me that I haven't come to see her for a while. Whoever tried to grab me took my phone, and apparently she's been trying to call my cell all day, even though she knows I work and can't answer. Then she accused me of changing my number and not telling her. Of course, she thinks I told George what it was. Her typical drunken ramblings."

"I'm sorry. I really wish I was there. I'm glad my brother's looking after you, though. Trust him to do that. He's not going to let anything happen to you."

"I'll admit he did talk me down from the ledge earlier tonight in your driveway."

"My driveway? Like, at our house? What are you doing there?"

"Your brother didn't tell you?"

"Tell me what?"

"I'm staying here for a bit. At least until they find the person who tried to grab me. I'm sleeping in your room, in fact. It was either this or a safe house while they try and figure out who's behind yesterday."

Ines was quiet.

"You still there?" I asked.

"Sorry, yeah, I'm here. I was just thinking about the fact that you and Victor are staying in the same house together, sleeping practically next door to each other."

My blood heated. I'd been trying to avoid thinking about

that exact thing from the moment Victor suggested I stay here. Ines suddenly burst into laughter.

"Oh my god. You and Victor are actually living in the same house. You two are either going to kill each other or kiss each other. I vote for the latter."

Damn Ines for putting that image in my head. Not that it wasn't already there.

"Never gonna happen. Well the killing might."

She snorted in disbelief. "Really? This is me you're talking to, Estelle. We've been friends almost my entire life. I've caught you staring at Victor over the years when you didn't think anyone was looking. I don't mean staring daggers either. I'm talking looks of longing."

I shifted. "It doesn't mean anything."

"It could. I know there's something between you two. Or at least the potential is there. You both have feelings you're afraid to admit."

Damn it. Why were we having this discussion now of all times? "Fine. I'll admit I'm attracted to Victor. It doesn't mean I'm going to do anything about it. Kissing can lead to more than kissing. More than kissing can lead to falling in love. And you know I don't believe in love."

"First of all, I didn't say anything about love. Only kissing. It doesn't necessarily *have to* lead to more than kissing. I know your parents did a number on you, but don't let their shitty marriage and bitter divorce sour you on romance. It does exist. Just look at Brody and me."

"You two are one of the rare exceptions. I have no desire to put that much trust in anyone. To open myself up to bitter hatred like my parents have. Besides, Victor and I argue like crazy. I listened to my parents argue and fight for most of my life. Hell, they still fight and continue to put me in the middle. No thank you. Why would I torture myself like that?"

"It's not the same and you know it. You argue with Victor to keep him at arm's length to protect yourself. Your parents do it because they hate each other. You and I both know you don't hate Victor."

"Doesn't matter. I have no desire to fall in love. I'm happy for you, and I know Brody makes you happy, but that's just not in the cards for me. Look, I don't want to talk about it anymore, okay? Why don't you tell me how you guys are doing?"

Ines, being my best friend, knew me well enough to let it go. That didn't mean the conversation wouldn't come up again, but her sigh told me she accepted current defeat.

"We're fine. Just bought a new bull who's giving Brody a little bit of trouble. He keeps busting through the fence to try and reach the heifers. I guess he's feeling frisky."

I snorted. I could picture Ines chasing down this giant cow with a broom trying to shoo him away from the ladies.

"Anyway," she continued. "We're staying busy with the ranch, that's for sure. Other than that just impatiently waiting until it's safe to come visit. I know Brody's going to reach out to his former handler at the D.E.A., Landon, especially in light of yesterday. The D.E.A. is no doubt looking for Álvarez in order to extradite him and bring him back for trial."

"Don't do anything that would put yourselves in danger. Like you said, I'm here with Victor. We'll be okay. Between him, your brothers, and your father, I'm well protected."

"I'm glad you're staying at the house. It does make me feel better. I really do miss you though."

"Same."

I glanced up to see Victor stepping back into the room tapping his wrist to indicate my time was up.

"Hey, I have to get going. It isn't safe to be on the phone much longer. Take care and tell Brody I send my regards. I love you."

"I love you too."

"Bye."

I disconnected the call and rose to hand the phone back to him.

"Sorry you couldn't talk longer." He stuck it in his pocket.

"I'm just glad I got to speak to her at all. Thank you for knowing I needed that."

He shrugged as though it weren't a big deal. Except it was. "You guys are best friends, and today was a struggle. I figured it was important for you to talk to her."

"I appreciate it so much."

"Happy to help. My dad should be home soon. Do you want to watch some TV for a bit?"

I glanced at the clock on the wall. "I better not. It's getting late, and I still have lesson plans I need to go over."

Victor seemed almost disappointed. "Of course. Also, I wanted you to know I'll take you to the school, but Pablo is going to pick you up. I have to work. Make sure you stay inside until he calls and tells you he's in the parking lot."

I saluted. "You got it."

He opened his mouth and then closed it again. There was a brief pause. "Well, have a good night and holler if you need anything."

"I will."

I grabbed my bag from the side table right inside the den, went up to my room, and closed the door. An hour later I was still sitting cross-legged in the middle of the bed. I'd barely made it through half my plans, because I couldn't stop thinking about Ines' words and kissing Victor.

Would his lips be soft and smooth? Or just a little rough from the scruff surrounding them? I imagined his kiss would be a lot like him. Playful and fun but also sexy and strong. I fell backwards onto the bed with a groan. I didn't want to be thinking about Victor or his kisses. It didn't matter that I'd been thinking of him since I was sixteen. In the end, it wouldn't work between us anyway. We were just too different.

CHAPTER 8

I STARED out the patrol car window, my gaze unfocused on the passing scenery while Gladstone chatted next to me. My mind hadn't been on work all day. All I could think about was Estelle. I'd dropped her off this morning with the reminder to wait for Pablo's call before leaving the school. Still, I was nervous about someone else, even my brother, picking her up and making sure she stayed safe.

"Yo, earth to Victor. You there man?"

"Hmmm?" I shook my head and turned to him. "What?"

My partner glanced at me with narrowed eyes. "What's going on with you today? You seem a little out of it."

My concentration was so off even Gladstone noticed.

"Just thinking."

"Does it have anything to do with the chick from a couple days ago? The one that almost got snatched out in the parking lot of that school."

My hackles raised. "Her *name* is Estelle."

His eyes darted in my direction before before he returned his attention back to the road. "Hey, no offense man. So...

does it have something to do with *Estelle*? I mean, how do you guys even know each other?"

"She's Ines' best friend."

"Ah," he drew out the word. "I see."

I looked at him with a narrow-eyed glare. There had been something in his tone.

"What does that mean?"

"What does what mean?"

"That little 'I see'."

Gladstone stopped at the stop sign before easing the patrol car onto Congress Street. "I just mean you were quick to jump in and offer for her to come stay with you guys is all. That's not really protocol."

"We didn't have a concrete suspect or motive. A safe house was overkill. It just made sense for her to go ahead and come to our house."

Gladstone smirked. "You're full of shit. You know that, right? I saw how you looked at her. Like she was a hot meal and you hadn't eaten for days."

"Jesus, Jonathan. She's a person, for god's sake, not some slab of meat."

"Whatever, man." he shrugged, unapologetically.

I turned away from him and looked out the window as we patrolled the streets. My partner had hit a nerve. Several of them in fact. It really wasn't protocol. But Estelle needed protection, and I didn't trust anyone else to provide it. I remained tense until Pablo called and said he'd picked up Estelle and delivered her safely to our house.

IT WAS after midnight before I finally walked through the

front door. I was surprised to see my dad sitting in his favorite leather recliner watching TV. He wasn't usually up this late, which had me a little worried.

"*Hola, m'hijo.*"

"*Hola, papá.*"

"Everything go okay on shift today?"

I took a seat on the edge of the sofa near him. "Yes, sir. Arrested a couple kids for possession. Answered a couple domestic disturbance calls, but other than writing a few tickets, it was a relatively slow day."

"That's good."

I hesitated. "How's Estelle?"

"She is fine."

I shifted uncomfortably under his stare. I'd never been able to hide anything from him. His quiet demeanor was also making me nervous. My father always had something to say so his succinct responses made me nervous. *Was he waiting for me to say more?* I wasn't sure I was ready to talk about things right now. I rubbed my palms on my pant legs and made to stand up and say my goodnight. My dad's next words stopped me.

"Got a call from Captain Petty today."

I lowered myself back onto the couch. "About?"

"Raúl Escobar is dead."

"Why do I know that name?"

"He was the Juárez Cartel's supplier down in Mexico. Alejandro and he were the ones who'd planned on overthrowing Álvarez. He was there the night Brody's cover was blown. It was his man who'd recognized him."

I ran my hands through my hair. "*Mierda.* Do we know who killed him?"

"Rumor has it… Álvarez. He has never taken kindly to betrayal, according to Brody."

My mind raced thinking about all the implications of this new development. "But if Escobar is dead, then who's his new supplier?"

"That's the problem. No one knows. At least not anyone at the local level. Whether or not the Feds or the D.E.A. know is another story. You know they're not going to talk to us. The only person who might even be able to get some intel is Brody."

"Which means he needs to talk to his handler and see what she'll tell him. He gave up that life. Is it fair to ask him to get involved again?"

"Fair or not, it's probably the only way."

"You may be right. I don't like it though. The more people he talks to the greater the chance the cartel discovers he's alive."

My father and I both remained quietly thinking. The consequences would be deadly. Not only for him, but also for my sister. I had to think about Estelle though. It was a no-win situation.

"Well there's nothing we can do right this second. Maybe once we sleep on it we'll think of something."

"Hopefully." My father didn't seem convinced.

"If there wasn't anything else, I'm going to head to bed." I made to stand again, but my father's words stopped me.

"Talk to me about Estelle, *m'hijo*."

I kept my expression blank. "I'm not sure what you mean."

He smiled knowingly at me. "You are my son, Victor. You may be able to lie to yourself, but you cannot lie to me. You have feelings for her."

"I don't know what I have, *papá*. Even if I did know, it wouldn't matter. Estelle doesn't particularly care for me. Besides, she's Ines' friend, and I wouldn't want to do anything that might jeopardize their friendship."

This time it was my father who rose. He put his hand on my shoulder. I looked up to see him staring down at me with such love.

"You have always been my most persistent child. Even more so than Ines. You've fought hard for what you've wanted, and you haven't let anything get in your way. When you really want something, then you do what it takes to get it. Just think on that. Sleep well, *m'hijo. Te amo.*"

"*Te amo, papá,*" I whispered.

Long after my father disappeared upstairs, I remained on the couch thinking. He'd been right. I did have feelings for Estelle. They'd started that day outside Ines' room. It was like a switch had been flipped. They'd grown and changed gradually. But they were there. My father was also right about me fighting for what I wanted. Was I up to the task of fighting against Estelle's resistance though?

CHAPTER 9

SATURDAYS WERE USUALLY my favorite day of the week. I got to sleep in, do a little yoga, go grocery shopping. Not today though. Today, I was stuck inside the house. Bored. We'd followed the same routine for the last two days. Victor took me to work, and someone picked me up. Honestly it was beginning to drive me crazy. I hated being dependent on anyone. I'd been doing things for myself since I was twelve, and I hadn't needed anyone's help yet. Even though I'd been going to work everyday, it wasn't the same. There I kept busy. A quick glance at the clock confirmed it was barely noon, and I was already developing cabin fever.

There was a big difference between not *wanting* to go somewhere and not being *able* to.

My lesson plans for the week were almost done, but I couldn't seem to sit still long enough to actually finish them. My legs kept twitching with the need to get up and move around. Thankfully, the rumble from my stomach told me it was time to take a break. It was pointless to keep sitting here, accomplishing nothing, so I tromped down the stairs for something to eat.

The kitchen was empty. I'd been a constant visitor here growing up and never felt awkward about helping myself.

I grabbed an apple, a leftover gordita, and a bit of cheese from the fridge and stacked them on a plate before heading into the living room. I curled up on the couch, tucked my feet underneath me, and pulled out the mystery novel I'd started reading a week ago but hadn't picked up in a few days. I flipped the pages and nibbled on my snacks, becoming thoroughly engrossed in my story. The front door opened just as I'd just popped the last piece of cheese in my mouth. Victor strode in. He caught sight of me and paused.

"Oh, hey. I didn't expect to see you down here. How's it going?"

Where else would I be? I swallowed. "Okay, I guess. A little restless. I'm not used to being cooped up all day."

"Yeah, sorry about that."

"I was hoping maybe I could get out of the house. At least for a little while."

Victor rubbed the back of his neck, like he was gearing himself up to say no, which annoyed me. It felt like I was asking for permission, even if, technically, I was.

"We might be able to go out for a bit. Where'd you want to go?"

"I meant by myself, but I should have known that wasn't going to be an option."

"Sorry, it's just not safe yet."

"I know. It was wishful thinking. I'd say let's get something to eat, but I just finished lunch." I gestured to my clean plate.

"Well, you haven't had dessert yet. Why don't we get some ice cream? A new place just opened up not too far from here."

If there was one thing I couldn't resist, it was ice cream. My desire to get out of the house had nothing to do with being stuck in here in general. It was more being stuck in the house with Victor. His constant presence was driving me crazy, because I couldn't stop thinking about him. I'd even started dreaming about him. The lure of my favorite dessert was too much, though, so I caved.

"Fine, but you're going to have to pay, since I don't have my wallet."

One side of his mouth tipped up. "So, if I'm paying, does this mean it's a date?"

I wrinkled my nose. "Not hardly."

Victor tilted his head and tapped a finger to his lips. "I don't know, it kind of sounds like a date to me."

I crossed my arms and barely refrained from stomping my foot. "It's definitely not."

"How badly do you want to get out of the house?" he asked with a devilish smile.

Aghast, I stared. "Are you seriously trying to blackmail me into saying this is a date?"

"All you have to do is say those three little words, and we'll walk out the front door."

This time, I did stomp my foot. "You are such a jerk."

Victor merely continued smiling. It made my heart skip. I threw my hands up in disgust with a groan. "I hate you. You know that, right?"

He outright laughed at this. "Nah, you just love ice cream that much. Come on, it'll be fun."

"Says the blackmailer."

Looping his hand through the crook of my elbow, he gently tugged me forward. My arms uncrossed and I expected him to release me. Instead he clasped my hand in his. I attempted to pull free, but he merely held a little tighter, refusing to let go. My skin tingled from his touch. Could he feel my swiftly beating pulse?

I gave up and let Victor lead me outside, because my desperation to get out of the house for a bit far outweighed my annoyance with him. A short drive later, my irritation had waned. I could also still feel the imprint of his warm hand against mine.

We stood at the counter waiting to order. Victor turned to me. "You going with mint chocolate chip, or something different today?"

Surprise flittered through me. "What makes you think I'd order mint chocolate chip?"

Victor looked at me like I was asking if the sky was blue. "Considering that's all you ever ate at our house, I assume that's the only ice cream you like. Or it's at least your favorite."

Stunned, I could only mumble. "Yeah, that's what I'm getting."

As though nothing profound just occurred, Victor moved up and placed our order while I stumbled forward, shell-shocked, to stand next to him. How did he remember my favorite flavor after all these years? Still a little dumbstruck, I took the cone he handed me and followed him to a back table in the corner. He sat facing the door while I took the seat opposite.

"How's yours?" he asked after a couple minutes.

"Oh, um, it's good."

"I never understood how people could enjoy the flavor of mint and chocolate together, but to each her own."

After glancing at his concoction of blue, pink, and purple flavors, I didn't think he had the right to be questioning my taste in ice cream. I looked up at him and my lips quirked. Victor licked his cone and stuck his tongue out at me. If nothing else he made me laugh and enjoy my time out of the house. Soon we'd both finished.

"So what made you go into teaching?"

I dabbed the napkin across my mouth. "I like working with kids, and I want to be able to provide a good education for them."

He studied me, and I tried not to squirm under his penetrating gaze. "That's a perfectly reasonable response. Too bad it sounded just a little too pat. C'mon, Bubbles, fess up. What's the real reason? Not the standard response you'd tell a stranger."

I didn't like that he could see right through me. My annoyance was pretty clear, because Victor softened his voice.

"Hey, this is me. You can trust me with the truth."

Could I though? I wanted to trust somebody, but I'd always held back so much of myself from everyone in my life. I didn't think I was, or would ever be, ready to fully trust anyone. Not even Victor. I wanted to believe so badly though. Taking a risk, I gave him what he asked for. The truth.

"All the time I spent at your house as a kid was because I was hiding from my parents. Well, I guess I wasn't so much hiding as much as avoiding them. They did nothing but scream and argue with each other until finally they got a divorce. You'd have thought it would end there, but it didn't."

I paused and remembered how happy I'd been after they split up. No kid should be glad their parents weren't together any longer.

"After the divorce, it just got worse, because then they used me to play games against the other. I was nothing but a pawn, a tool, in a war I wanted no part of. Being a teacher gives me the ability to make sure that each and every kid who steps through my classroom door feels special. Loved. Especially if they're not getting that at home. It was the best way I knew I could do that."

Victor reached across the table and laid his hand over mine.

"Based on what I saw that first day in your classroom, you've done exactly that. I could instantly tell how much you love those kids. How much they love you, as well. You should be proud. Any kid would be lucky to have you for their teacher." He was so earnest, I actually believed him.

"Thank you for saying that."

"I'm only speaking the truth."

We stared at each other, Victor's warm hand clasping mine. Everything around us faded away, and it was just the two of us sitting here. It was like I was seeing him for the first time. I was acutely aware of his thumb caressing my knuckles, and it sent a warm, tingling sensation up my arm to settle low in my belly. I didn't want this feeling of contentment to go away, but I knew it wouldn't last. Nothing ever did.

Knowing I'd let it go on for too long, I slid my hand from beneath his and dropped it into my lap with my other one.

Victor frowned. "Why do you do that?"

"Do what?"

"Pull away and shut down."

There wasn't any point in denying what he said. "I have no desire to be another in a long line of conquests. I'm not exactly sure what it is you want from me, but I know I can't give it to you."

CHAPTER 10

It STUNG to hear Estelle's low opinion of me. While I was by no means a monk, I certainly wasn't the man-whore she seemed to think I was.

"That is entirely presumptuous. If you don't know what I want, which, by the way, is not another 'conquest'," —I emphasized with air quotes— "whatever that means, how do you know you can't give it to me?"

"How many long-term relationships have you been in?"

I drew back. "I don't know what that has to do with anything."

"Just answer the question."

"Fine. I haven't been in any."

"Exactly," Estelle said emphatically as though that proved some point she was trying to make. "You're twenty-eight years old, and you've never been in a single one. Ines has told me stories about all the different women you've dated. Who've come and gone through a revolving door."

For a brief second, I swore she sounded jealous. A light bulb went off.

"You're jealous."

She scoffed. "Not hardly."

"You are. You're also wrong. Date doesn't mean fuck. I've dated plenty of women I've never slept with. The ones I did, I wouldn't call conquests. And the only thing I'm asking you for is a chance."

"A chance at what? For you to break my heart?"

I sat forward, rested my forearms on the table, and lowered my voice. "What happens if you break mine? Have you ever thought about that?"

Estelle didn't say anything. She merely worried her lip.

"Look, I'm not asking for anything more than taking the time to really get to know each other."

"Where's this suddenly coming from? We don't even like each other."

My eyes locked onto hers. "You and I both know this isn't sudden. It's been brewing just below the surface for the last ten years. Waiting to be acknowledged. I can also guarantee that we like each other more than either of us have ever admitted."

I sank back against my chair. Finally, after all these years I actually put it out there. It was freeing to admit there had been something there, simmering between us all this time. Like my father said, when I wanted something, I went after it. It was time Estelle understood that she was who I wanted. I knew she wouldn't make it easy for me.

I couldn't push her though. If there was one thing I'd observed about Estelle over the years, it was that she was stubborn. The last thing I wanted to do was push her even further away.

"You don't have to give me an answer today. Just think

about it." I glanced at my watch and saw the time. "We should get going."

I gave her some space as we walked to the truck.

"Thanks for getting me out of the house for a bit. I really do appreciate it," Estelle said quietly once we were on the road.

"You're welcome."

She stared out the window after that. I hoped it was because she was thinking on everything I'd said. Turning my attention back to my surroundings, I glanced into the rearview mirror in time to see a black SUV directly on my ass. *Shit, he was going to hit us.*

"Hold on," I yelled and braced myself for impact.

My head snapped forward and a searing pain shot up my neck. I gripped the steering wheel hard to maintain control.

"You okay?" I shouted at Estelle, looking back and forth between the road in front of me and the reflection in the mirror of the vehicle behind us.

"I'm fine."

"Damn it. He's going to do it again." I spared a quick glance in the side mirror. I jerked the wheel hard to the right, prayed no one was in my blind spot, and slammed on the gas pedal. I continued with several more evasive measures, but the vehicle stuck right on my tail. Tires squealed as I skidded around the next turn and headed toward the police station only a few blocks away.

"Reach into my pocket and get my cell phone."

With only a second of hesitation, Estelle did as I asked. I raised a hip to give her better access.

"Call Manuel. We're in his precinct, and near his station house. Tell him what's going on."

Without waiting to see if she followed my instructions, I

made several quick turns down city streets. What crazy bastard tried to ram a vehicle, a truck especially, in the middle of the day?

I could hear Estelle on the phone while I kept my eyes on the vehicle behind us. *Were they slowing down?* Everything happened at once. My truck spun from the impact of something crashing into the driver's side. The screech of metal against metal and Estelle's scream echoed through the air. My entire body jerked to the right, and glass shattered around me. Stinging pain pelted the side of my face. I slammed my foot on the brake, and we came to a screeching halt.

I shook my head to clear the dizziness and blurry vision. *Fuck. Estelle?* My gaze shot to her.

"Estelle, baby, are you okay? Estelle?"

She groaned. *Goddammit.*

I looked out the windshield. We were smack dab in the middle of the street, sitting cross ways, blocking the flow of traffic in both directions. I unclipped my seatbelt. Wincing, I jerked open the glove compartment and pulled out my gun.

My head swiveled from side to side as I looked out. There were lines of stopped cars on either side of us. There was no sign of the black SUV or of whatever vehicle hit us.

"Is everyone all right?"

I jerked my arm up and pointed the gun at the face peering through the hole where my window used to be. The man leapt backward with his hands up.

"Whoa, hey now, I'm just making sure you guys are okay. I called 9-1-1, and the police and paramedics are on their way."

Ignoring the man, I turned back to Estelle. She shifted

and moaned in pain as she reached up to cup her head. Gently, I laid my hand on her arm.

"Talk to me, honey. You okay?"

She slowly turned toward me, and I cursed at the blood dripping down the side of her face.

"What happened?" Her voice trembled.

"Someone rammed into us. Sit tight, baby, help is on the way."

The sound of sirens grew louder. I placed the gun back in the glove box and yanked my shirt up and over my head. I leaned across the middle console toward Estelle.

"Here, move your hand."

I pressed my shirt against her forehead to try and slow the bleeding. She sucked in a sharp breath. Out of the corner of my eye I caught sight of blue flashing lights.

"You're safe now. No one is going to hurt you again."

"Shit, Victor, are you guys all right?" My head snapped to the side, and over my shoulder I spotted my brother, Manuel, standing outside the vehicle. I saw the fear in his expression.

"I'm fine, I think, but Estelle's hurt. She's got a head wound that's bleeding like a motherfucker. We need an ambulance."

"One's on its way."

I turned back to her. "Hold this tight, right there. I'll be right back."

"Victor?" She trembled in fear, and I cupped her jaw. "I'm just coming around to your side. I'm not going anywhere. I promise."

She nodded. Once I saw her put pressure on the makeshift bandage, I jumped out of the truck, practically pushing my brother out of the way, and raced to the other side of the truck. The panicky sensation in my gut wouldn't go away until I knew Estelle was taken care of. I opened her door, trying to remain calm, but seeing so much blood on her face had rage and fear running like wildfire through my veins.

She turned toward me.

"I'm here. See?"

I replaced her hand hold on my shirt with my own and cupped her cheek with my free hand. I needed to touch her and reassure myself that she was all right. Whoever was responsible for hurting her was going to pay.

I don't know if she sensed how on edge I was, but she laid her hand over mine. "I'm okay, Victor. It probably looks worse than it is."

"What happened?" Manuel asked from behind me.

I'd completely forgotten he was here. My eyes didn't leave Estelle's. "We'd just left Cold Scoops and were on our way home when a black SUV rear-ended us. I tried losing them, but they stayed on my tail. I was headed to your station house, which is why I had Estelle call you. Out of nowhere, somebody tore through the intersection and side-swiped us."

"Did you get a look at the vehicle that hit you?"

I shook my head. "No, it all happened too fast. It had to have been big, though, to knock out my truck like that."

More sirens blared and soon an ambulance pulled up. Two paramedics jumped out. They swarmed us with their medical equipment, and I reluctantly stepped away from Estelle so they could assist her.

I stood, helplessly, running my hands through my hair, frustrated I couldn't do more to help.

"I'm going to take a look and see what we got going on here." He pulled my shirt away from her face.

Each time she winced, a stabbing pain shot through my heart. She could have been killed today.

"It looks like the bleeding has already slowed."

I watched the paramedic clean off the blood and tape a piece of gauze over the wound. Once he was done, he packed up all his supplies and stepped away. In an instant, I took his place next to Estelle.

"The bandage should do for now, but you hit your head pretty hard. Why don't we get you over to the hospital, so you can get checked out better. Make sure you don't have a concussion."

"No, I don't want to go to the hospital."

"Este—" I started.

She grabbed my hand. "I'm fine. Please."

I sighed but turned to the paramedic. "She doesn't want to go. We appreciate your help though."

The paramedic studied me and then nodded.

"Don't get the bandage wet for at least twelve hours. If you get headaches or blurred vision, you really should see your doctor."

Estelle nodded. "I will."

He and his partner returned to the ambulance and left the scene. Several more police vehicles showed up.

Manuel moved closer to me. "I'll stay here with you until the tow truck comes and then I'll take you guys home."

"Thanks," I nodded, absently before turning to Estelle. "You feeling well enough to stand up?"

"I think so."

She clasped my hand, and I helped her down from the

truck. Her steps stuttered, and I pulled her to me. Those fuckers were going to pay for hurting her.

"I've got you."

Manuel pointed toward his police cruiser. "Here, she can sit in my car."

With Estelle held tight against my side, I helped her over to the vehicle and settled her in the back seat, my blood still raging hot with a fiery vengeance. I hovered over her while other cops came and took a formal statement. The tow truck also came and loaded my truck onto its platform.

"Come on. I'll take you guys home," Manuel said when the truck was out of sight.

"Thanks."

It was a quiet drive with Estelle resting against my shoulder. She hadn't resisted when I put my arm around her. I needed her close, so I knew she was okay.

We pulled up in front of the house, and Manuel opened the back door for us.

"I'll let Dad know what happened when I get back to the station. Take care of her. We'll call a family meeting tomorrow when everyone's around."

I nodded absently and guided Estelle inside. My brother was right. She could have been killed today. I needed to do a better job of protecting her.

CHAPTER 11

MY HEAD WAS THROBBING, and all I wanted to do was take some pain relievers and lie down. I don't think I'd ever been so scared in my entire life. Even now, my body trembled a little. Victor led me into the house. It felt good to have someone to lean on, even if it was only temporary.

Considering how much my head was pounding, I was grateful for his help. We got to the top of the stairs and stopped in front of Ines' room.

"I want to get the rest of that blood cleaned off you. Let me throw a shirt on real quick. Will you be okay right here?"

I nodded. "I'm fine."

He disappeared into his room and reappeared less than a minute later pulling a navy t-shirt over his head.

"Come on." Victor spoke softly, leading me into the bathroom.

He boosted me onto the counter and I squeaked, grabbing his forearms in surprise. He reached into the medicine cabinet and pulled out a white bottle with a red label. Then he handed me two pills and a cup of water.

"You're probably needing these, I bet."

"Thank you. My head is killing me."

"I bet. I'll take you to the ER tonight if it's not any better."

He ran the water again and grabbed a washcloth. The temperature must have met with his satisfaction, because he soaked the cloth in it. He stepped between my legs, and I froze. With a finger, he gently turned my head to the side.

"Close your eyes."

They fluttered shut, and he tenderly wiped away the remaining dried blood from my face with the warm cloth. His chest brushed against my breasts, and I stopped breathing. My nipples puckered at the touch. He rinsed out the cloth and re-warmed it several more times. I could feel his breath on my cheek and his muscled chest against mine.

"It's as clean as it's going to get. I don't want to rub too hard or get your bandage wet."

Slowly, I opened my eyes. Victor stared at me with an intensity that made my heart race and my face burn. He brushed my hair off my face and tucked it behind my ear. I couldn't tear my eyes away from his.

"I'm sorry you were hurt today." His voice was low.

"It wasn't your fault," I replied just as softly. I didn't want to disturb this intimacy between us.

Victor's gaze glided over my face and with the softest touch, he stroked the area around my bandage, taking care not to brush over it. Goose bumps pebbled my arms.

"You're going to have quite the shiner."

Self-consciously, I shifted. "I'm sure I look a mess."

He caressed my cheek. A shiver dashed across the back of my neck. I wanted to lean into his touch so bad, but I held myself still.

"You're beautiful, no matter what." His voice washed over me like a warm blanket covering me with its heat.

"You don't have to say that."

"Since when do I say something I don't mean? I've thought you were beautiful since you were sixteen. Your eyes are blue like the Caribbean, and when you smile, it lights up the room."

I ducked my head, feeling suddenly shy. I didn't realize Victor was a romantic.

My eyes raised to meet his again, and I bit my lip nervously. "Thank you."

His gaze locked on my mouth, and his brown eyes darkened. His nostrils flared. *Could he smell my need?* This was crazy. We could have been killed today. I should not be turned on right now. But was I ever.

"You're welcome."

Victor helped me down from the counter, breaking the spell. "How's your head doing?"

I squashed my disappointment before taking stock of my body. Surprisingly, my headache had eased. "It's actually feeling better."

"Good. Why don't you go get some rest? I need to make some phone calls."

Victor squeezed my hand before leaving me outside my bedroom. I watched him descend the stairs, and then I closed myself in my room. I collapsed with a sigh against the door. *What the hell just happened back there?*

Suddenly, exhaustion hit me, or, most likely, the shock was wearing off. Either way, I toed off my shoes, and fell onto the bed fully dressed. Almost the second my head hit the pillow, I was out.

THE PRESSING need to relieve my bladder woke me up. I laid in bed a few more minutes not quite ready to get up. There was barely any light left peeking through the slats of the mini blinds. *Great, now I'll never sleep tonight.* My head twinged a bit which gave me another reminder that it was time to get moving.

I took care of business and while I was washing my hands I glanced at my reflection in the mirror. Damn, Victor was right. My face was already starting to bruise. I was also reminded of what occurred in here a few short hours ago. Along with our conversation at Cold Scoops. Did I dare take a chance at letting Victor get close? I had no intention of falling in love. It didn't mean we couldn't spend time together though.

I took one more glance in the mirror, my decision made. Now to find Victor. My search led me to the den. I stood for a few moments observing him. Dark hair he kept cut close because otherwise his curls got out of control. The olive complexion and brown eyes. He had a jawline hid by the scruff he'd grown, but I could still recall the sharp angles of it. I'd dreamed about that face for years.

His looks weren't all that drew me to him. He was a great brother to Ines. They'd always been close, and he'd encouraged her when she'd wanted to follow in the family footsteps and become a police officer. He was charming when he wanted to be. While I'd never tell him, he had a great sense of humor and always made me laugh.

He glanced up from his computer. My heart skipped at the smile he sent my way.

"Hey there. How're you feeling?" He rose from the chair to stand in front of me. His gaze scanned my wound.

Before I could stop myself, I took a step forward and rose up onto my tiptoes. My hands landed on Victor's chest to support myself. It took everything I had not to curl my fingers into his shirt and tug him closer. Instead I just barely brushed my lips across his before pulling back slightly. Our breath mingled and our mouths still practically touched. I locked eyes with him.

"Thank you for taking care of me," I murmured against his lips.

He pulled me tight against him, and I sucked in a breath. I followed his every move as he tilted his head and, with breathtaking slowness, lowered his mouth to mine. This was no gentle brushing of lips. His tongue traced the seam of my mouth. I opened to him, and he plundered it as though trying to find a buried treasure. He tasted me. Devoured me. There was no holding anything back.

Victor consumed me.

His hair was soft between my fingertips as I clutched him tightly to me. I was punch drunk on his taste. His scent infused itself deep inside me. Musk and man. All Victor.

Our tongues danced, and I lost all track of time. My hips burned from the touch of his hands. His grip was strong and only made me want to discover how powerful and talented his hands really were. I was so swept away in delirious sensation, I almost missed the sound of someone clearing his throat. When it sounded again, only louder, Victor and I broke apart. Both of us were breathing heavy.

"Sorry to interrupt, but I figured you'd want to know that dad's about to walk through the front door in about thirty seconds. You might want to" —Pablo gestured vaguely with a finger in our direction— "take that some-where else besides the family den."

I glanced down and saw my shirt was half pushed up. Almost far enough to expose my bra. Quickly, I yanked it down and smoothed it over my belly while avoiding Pablo's gaze. My entire body flushed, and I was ready to dig a hole and crawl in it.

"Thanks for the heads up."

I glanced over at the amusement in Victor's tone. He looked down at me and had the gall to wink.

"Based on the evil eye Estelle's throwing your way, bro, you might want to tone down your charm. While you two do what you do best, I'm going to my room. Call me when dinner's ready." Pablo turned and disappeared down the hallway.

Once he was gone, I looked back at Victor. "What are you staring at?"

His expression had turned serious. "I'm not staring. I'm thinking."

"Don't hurt yourself," I tossed the words out, doing what, like Pablo said, I did best. Keep Victor at arm's length. I spun on my heels and started to head upstairs.

Victor grabbed my hand. "Wait. Where are you going?"

I avoided his gaze. "To my room. I have work I need to finish."

"Aren't we going to talk about what just happened?"

Not if I could help it. I shrugged. "It was only a kiss, Victor."

"Goddamn it, Estelle, this is exactly what I'm talking about. The minute I try to get close, you pull away."

I avoided his knowing gaze. The one that saw right

through me. "I'm not pulling away. I told you, I have work to do. Besides, I'm not sure what there is to talk about."

He held up his hands like he didn't understand why I was even asking. It didn't help matters that I was now just as confused as him.

"Oh, I don't know. How about everything that happens next, maybe?"

I wrapped my arms around myself and stared at the wall over his shoulder.

"I don't know what happens next. But I do know I'm not ready to talk about it." With that, I made my exit, scurrying away like a scared little mouse. Which was exactly what I was. In fact, I was terrified if I were being honest. I'd had my mind made up to test the waters. Spend time together. Get to know each other. I'd also still planned on guarding my heart. That was before his lips touched mine. Because that kiss? That kiss changed everything.

CHAPTER 12

"Son of a bitch." I slammed my fists against my thighs.

"*M'hijo*, is everything okay?" My father stood in the hallway, concern evident on his face.

I dropped into the recliner, my head hanging in a mixture of defeat and frustration. "I pushed too hard, I think, *papá*."

My father moved across the room and sat on the edge of the couch. "Let me tell you a story. One night, when Ines was eight or nine, I received a phone call. It was late evening, perhaps around ten. I could barely make out the words behind the tears of the little girl on the other end. The screaming and loud crashes in the background didn't help. After a time, I was able to calm her down enough to understand what she was saying."

I sat upright. He was talking about Estelle. My father stared hard at me like what he was about to impart something extremely important.

"I told her to lock herself in the bathroom, and I'd be right over. The screaming was still going on when I pounded on the front door fifteen some minutes later. Her father jerked the door open and berated me for knocking on his door so late, even though he knew who I was. I pushed past him and said I was taking the girl home with me for the evening." His voice hardened, and I could hear the anger in it as he continued his story.

"Tentatively, she peered around the corner, her large blue eyes sparkling with unshed tears. In her hands was a tattered teddy bear with several holes and white stuffing peeking out of them. I grabbed a blanket off the couch and wrapped it around her tiny body. I brought her home without a single word of resistance from either of her parents and tucked her in bed with your sister. The next morning I told her that she should always count on me being there whenever she needed me."

I sat there in stunned silence. I vaguely recalled waking up one day as a kid and finding Estelle in the house. She hadn't been there when I'd gone to bed. But it happened so long ago, I'd forgotten about it.

"That is the kind of family your Estelle grew up in. Two people who should have loved each other more than anything screaming and cursing at the other. They also didn't seem to care enough to protest the fact that I was leaving with their daughter. They only cared about their hatred for one another. For Estelle, that is what love represents. She fights so hard because if her love turned into what her parents had, it would destroy her. *That* is the memory you have to contend with."

Fuck. I knew it wouldn't be easy but not to this degree. It was a good thing I was a stubborn fucker. I was going to show her she could trust me, because Estelle was worth it. I rose and leaned down to kiss my father's cheek. "*Gracias, papá.* Thank you for telling me. You gave me a lot to think about."

"Just be patient, *m'hijo.* Show her every day how you feel. Don't be afraid to let her see your feelings."

"I wish you and mama had longer together."

"Your mother was an amazing woman. She was my soul mate. We had fifteen of the best years of my life together. Every day I'm grateful for the children we were blessed with. You, your brothers, and sister are her legacy. She would be proud of all of you."

I kissed his cheek again. *"Te amo, papá. Buenas noches."*

I went upstairs and paused for a beat outside Ines' room. Trying to give Estelle some more space, I didn't knock. Instead, I went to my room to plan.

IT WAS LATE, well after eleven. My cell phone rang just as I'd laid down.

"Hello?"

"Is this Victor?"

"Who's this?" I certainly wasn't going to confirm my identify to some random caller.

"A friend. You and I share two mutual friends who recently left the city for a more… can we say discreet location? With much more wide-open spaces and few neighbors."

I sat up and swung my legs off the side of the bed. My fingers tightened on the phone. The only person this could be was Preston Thomas. Why was Brody's brother calling me?

"What can I do for you?"

"I have a proposition for you, but I don't want to talk over the phone."

"Where?"

"Can you meet me in about an hour at Mickey's Bar? It's on the corner of Easton and Barber near Wicker Park."

"I'll be there."

"See you then."

After getting dressed, I opened up my closet and pulled the lock box down from the top shelf. I pounded out the combination and heard the lock disengage. From it, I withdrew my personal .35mm and clipped the holster onto my waistband. It wasn't necessarily that I didn't trust Brody's brother, but I'd rather go into a meeting prepared. The only thing I knew about him was he was a recovering heroin addict who'd been clean about a year.

I wasn't prepared to explain my destination to my father or brother yet. As quietly as possible I crept downstairs. I made it as far as the kitchen before I remembered my truck was out of commission. *Shit*. My only option was to take my father's car. I grabbed the keys off their hook and slipped out the front door. Before long, I stood inside the entrance of Mickey's Bar, my eyes scanning the dim, smoky room.

Straight down the middle were square tables, peppered here and there with older gentleman who stared just as intently back at me. Off to the right were a couple of pool tables with games in session. To the left was a fully stocked bar complete with a long, wall length mirror behind it reflecting the entire place. A bartender stood at the far end drying glasses. He greeted me with a chin jerk.

The main thing I noticed was that, while not a large crowd, everyone appeared near my dad's age. Was I at the right place? From the farthest back corner, a younger man around my age, slid out of one of the dark colored, tattered leather booths lining the back wall and strode toward me. He was tall, a little over six foot, with the sleeves of his shirt pushed up past his elbows.

"Victor?"

I nodded and held out my hand. "You must be Preston."

He shook my hand, and I couldn't help but notice the track marks dotting the inside of his elbows. He saw where my gaze landed but didn't try to hide them.

"Thanks for coming. Why don't we take a seat?" He gestured toward the booth he'd vacated.

I trailed after him. The penetrating gaze of multiple sets of eyes followed us, but no one made a move. Preston scooted into the booth, and I moved in opposite him. The faint sounds of country music seeped from the speakers of the nearby jukebox.

"So, what sort of proposition do you have in mind?" I broke the silence.

"I talked to Brody yesterday and heard what happened to Ines' friend. He also told me you guys are looking for information on the whereabouts of Miguel Álvarez. I've been thinking it over, and after a long and drawn out argument with my brother, I think I found a way to help you locate him. Or at least get information on where he might possibly be hiding."

"How do you think you can do that?" I was definitely skeptical.

Preston hesitated and then steeled his expression. He gestured to his exposed scars. "I'm sure you've heard about my drug addiction."

I inclined my head. "It might have been mentioned."

"Yes, I'm sure it has." His lips tipped up in one corner.

81

"I'm sure you're also aware that I'm one of the reasons Brody joined the D.E.A. and went undercover to bring down the cartel."

Actually, that bit of information surprised me, but I hid the fact. "I may have heard something to that effect as well."

I was now even more curious to see what his plan was.

"Although Brody says he's forgiven me, it's something I don't know that I can ever forgive myself for. Which is why it's important for me to find a way to help. I can never right the wrongs I've done, but I can do my damnedest to atone for them."

"Go on."

"I have connections in the drug world that you, as a cop, don't have. Dealers trust me. As much as they trust anybody that is. Addicts also talk. Usually about who has the best stash, which has always been Álvarez. Because I'm one of them, the chances of someone talking to me are far greater. They're also not suspicious about certain questions being asked. I'll get a lot farther than if you or your cop buddies ask them. Addicts have a special code. We don't narc."

Preston sat back and let all the information he'd just exposed sink in. If I was interpreting his words correctly, it sounded as though Brody's brother just offered to go against the entire code he was supposed to live by.

"How would what you're suggesting work?"

He sat forward again, his voice low. "You'd be my point of contact. I'd ask around, looking for the best stuff. Then I'd notify you when a deal was about to go down. After the trade, whether it be information or products, I'd hand everything off to you. With each deal, hopefully we'd move further up the food chain, which will then lead us to Álvarez."

In theory his plan sounded perfect, but the reality would be far different. Especially considering the fact that a recovering addict was going to be in possession, albeit briefly, of the very things he craved.

"I take it Brody didn't agree with this plan?"

Preston harrumphed. "Why would he? It's dangerous for so many reasons. My brother and I have had a…strained relationship over the last almost eleven years. Considering the life I've led, it's understandable. I don't blame him for his hesitation about me putting myself in situations that could cause my relapse. Although hesitant is putting it mildly. I think his exact words were 'Are you out of your fucking mind?'."

I had to laugh. But I also took pause. As someone with my own brotherly issues, I commiserated with Preston. I knew what it was like living in an older sibling's shadow.

"What happens if you can't get the information we're looking for?"

"I will." There was determination and confidence behinds words. "People talk. Especially those wanting a fix."

"What happens if you become one of those people? The one wanting a fix, I mean."

His laugh was hollow. "You must not know much about addicts. We're always wanting a fix. Some of us just realize there are things we want more."

"Like?"

"Like atonement."

CHAPTER 13

I'D TOSSED and turned the entire night reliving Victor's kiss. It was everything I'd thought it would be yet so much more. What I wouldn't give to be able to talk to Ines about this. On second thought, maybe that wasn't such a good idea. She'd tell me to pull my head out of my ass. She'd also be absolutely right.

I'd given up getting any sleep at seven this morning. Instead, I got up and went downstairs for a cup of coffee. The house had been quiet. The kitchen empty. It was the first time since my stay at the Rodriguez house began that no one had been milling around. It was a little disconcerting. The house had always been full of hustle and bustle. I filled my mug, grabbed an orange and banana, and had come back up to finish my lesson plans for the week. Now that that was done, I couldn't come up with any more reasons to stay hidden in my room.

"Ugh." I threw my head back in frustration. Why did life have to be so damn complicated? Why did I let my parents continue to have this stupid hold over me? They'd ruined so many things for me over the years. I couldn't let them ruin this too. I needed to talk to Victor.

What was the worst that could happen if we explored this... attraction between us? Aside from ending up with a broken heart and possibly losing my best friend that is? Ines wouldn't want to take sides, and I knew that could cause tension between her and Victor. More than anything, I didn't want that. I needed to re-evaluate my life though. Did I really want to spend the rest of it alone because I was afraid? Afraid to take a risk? Afraid of falling in love? Fuck.

I uncrossed my legs and threw them over the edge of the bed. For several minutes I sat there gathering my courage. With a determined heave, I pushed myself out the bedroom door and down the hall. Before I lost my courage, I knocked on Victor's door. I fidgeted, and continued questioning my decision, while I waited for him. The door opened, and my time for second guessing was over.

He stood in the half-opened doorway wearing nothing but a pair of low-slung jeans. My eyes locked on the narrow strip of hair that disappeared below his waistband. *Focus, Estelle.* I blinked and lifted my gaze back up to his face. His eyes were hooded, and I couldn't see what he was thinking. His cheeky grin was absent, and I sorely missed it.

"May I come in?"

Without a word, he stepped back. I swallowed hard and clutched my fingers tightly in front of me when he shut us both in. This was the first time I'd been in Victor's room. It wasn't anything like I'd imagined. His bed was perfectly made, the pillows tucked neatly beneath the folded over flap of a black down comforter. No clothes were strewn all over. Instead, there was a hamper in the corner.

A family portrait in a black frame hung on the wall above

his dresser. His gun belt lay neatly across the top of it along-side a set of car keys and a wallet. None of that really drew my eye, though. What did was the huge office desk and high back leather chair that took up at least a third of the room. Sitting on the desk were two gigantic computer monitors, side by side, with a paused video game on one screen and a chat display on the other. I didn't expect Victor to be a gamer. Certainly not one who played what looked like...*was that Spiderman?*

"Why are you here, Estelle?" Victor interrupted my perusal of his private space.

I turned to face him again and forced myself to look him in the eye. He deserved the truth. "I came to say you were right. I do push you away. It's been my defense mechanism for years. I don't let people close, because then I don't risk getting hurt."

With a deep inhale, I continued. "I also came to say I'm sorry. I'm sorry for running away last night. For being a coward. Mostly, I'm sorry for hurting you."

I braced myself when he stepped forward, but he merely moved past me without a word. Spinning around, I watched him run his hands over his head. A gesture I'd seen him do countless times when he was frustrated. His mussed hair made him look several years younger. My breathing was ragged as I pushed back my anxiety. I'd said what needed to be said, but I couldn't force him to accept my apology. My stomach ached with the tension between us. The air had never felt this heavy before. I lost track of how long I waited for him to respond. Finally, I couldn't take it any longer.

"Please, will you say something? Anything?"

He stood still, his profile to me when he spoke. "My entire life I've lived in the shadow of three older brothers.

They'd grown up together and had already formed a bond before I ever came along. I think that's why Ines and I were always so close. Being only a year and a half apart, it seemed like it was us against them."

He paused, his eyes staring into nothing like he was lost in the memories. He blinked and visibly shook them off. He shifted and his focus landed on me.

"Regardless, we could always rely on each other. If one of us needed something the others were quick to offer help. I don't know your whole story. Only a tiny piece of it. And that is you didn't have the kind of life or childhood we had. Even though you were here all the time. I never gave it much thought until recently."

Whether knowingly or not, Victor was picking at my scabbed wound that never fully healed. The whole reason I kept people from getting too close.

"I'm sorry for what you had to deal with as a kid. I have no doubt it tainted your view on what a healthy relationship should look like. They're not all like that, Estelle. *We* wouldn't be like that."

Victor was right. Wherever this thing between us went, we wouldn't wind up bitter and hating each other.

"I know," I whispered.

I didn't resist when he closed the distance between us and pulled me into his arms. I pressed closer, as though I could become a part of him. With my cheek against his chest, his heartbeat sounded loud. His scent surrounded me, comforting me. We both stood there, each of us silently holding the other. I absorbed the closeness, soaking it all up, so when I needed to, I could pull out the memory of this feeling of intimacy between us. I'd never had this before, and it was almost too much.

"We're going to take things slow. When you need time or space, we'll talk about it. I know you're scared. I am too." Victor's voice rumbled through my body to settle deep inside my soul.

"You're going to have to be patient with me. Most likely I'm going to be… difficult."

He chuckled above my head. "You've been difficult for more years than I can count. I'm still here aren't I?"

I pulled back to stare up at him. "You were awfully quick to agree with that."

He shrugged and gave me his half-smile. The one that always caused my belly to flutter. "I call 'em like I see them. Besides, there's nothing wrong with being difficult. Now that I know it's what you've done to protect yourself, I can work with it."

He cupped my jaw and caressed my cheek with his thumb. My breath hitched. I gave up the fight I'd always had with myself and leaned into his touch. For once, I needed someone to lean on.

"You can trust me to be here for you. Anytime you need me, all you have to do is ask."

"Well, it's not like you can go anywhere, since you kind of live here."

Things between Victor and I were suddenly getting too heavy. I needed the levity to counteract the vulnerability I was feeling. I still needed that little bit of space between us. Trust wasn't going to happen overnight. No matter how much I wanted it to. His expression shifted, and he sighed softly.

He might as well get used to it.

"I guess you're right." This time it was Victor who pulled away and took a few steps backward. The intimacy between us was broken, and it was my fault. The silence between us was awkward and uncomfortable. It was time for me to leave. "I should get going. I'm sure you have things you need to do."

"As a matter of fact, I don't."

I paused in my retreat. "Oh."

"Have you eaten lunch yet?"

I shook my head. "Not yet. I grabbed some coffee and fruit early this morning. Otherwise I've been finishing up my lesson plans for the week."

"Come on then. Let's go down and grab some lunch." Victor clasped my hand in his. I jerked the tiniest bit from the charge of electricity that zinged through my fingertips and up my spine. The look he shot me was almost one of daring. Daring me to pull away. I wasn't going to let him goad me. Instead I smiled my toothiest smile, all while praying he didn't notice the tremble of my sweating hand. Despite that tingle that still sizzled across my skin, I didn't release my hold on his fingers as we headed downstairs together.

CHAPTER 14

I PACED the length of the den while my father sat in his recliner. Manuel was, like usual, in the kitchen finding something to eat. You'd think his wife never fed him. Pablo should be here any minute for the family meeting Manuel had called yesterday after the accident. We needed to talk about what happened and what we needed to do to keep Estelle safe. There was no way that crash was random. It had to tie into the attempted kidnapping. I just didn't know how to prove it.

Manuel came in carrying a sandwich, his mouth already full. We all turned at the sound of a key hitting the lock. Pablo walked in. "Sorry I'm late."

"You're here now. That's all that matters," my father assured him.

He hung his gun belt near the door and joined us. "Any news about the crash yesterday?"

My father answered. "Nothing. We checked all the video surveillance in the area of surrounding businesses as well as traffic cams. They showed the whole collision happening, but the windows of both vehicles were tinted so dark it was impossible to get a clear glimpse of anyone inside."

He'd shared all this with me yesterday, but hearing it a second time pissed me off again.

"Both the SUV and the Hummer had stolen plates, so no help there," Manuel offered.

A fucking dead end. The APB on Álvarez had come up with nothing as of yet. We couldn't find anyone around town still on his payroll. Even our informants were batting zero. Which meant he was really good at hiding. Or he wasn't back in Chicago. He couldn't show his face for fear of getting arrested, but that didn't mean he wasn't here. If what Brody said was correct, he would do whatever it took to get his revenge. The only problem was that everything pointed to the fact I was grasping at straws at Álvarez being responsible for Estelle's attack. I needed someone to blame for what happened to her. It pissed me off that I couldn't get confirmation. I just needed something. A single lead.

"Brody's brother called me last night."

All eyes landed on me. I held up my hand to stop the barrage of questions that followed.

"He had a proposition for me."

"What sort of proposition?" My father asked.

"He's offered to help try and locate Álvarez."

Pablo spoke up from the position he'd taken on the couch. "Offered how? And is that really a good idea? We don't know anything about him."

This was where things were going to get dicey. "He's willing to become a narc."

"I think that needs further explaining, *m'hijo*."

"He says he can get information the police can't. Tips on where deals are taking place. Where to get the best drugs and who to get them from. We're going to work together in gathering intel."

"I don't like this," Manuel piped up.

I spun on him. "What don't you like? The fact that I'm the one he reached out to? Or that I might be the one who locates Álvarez?"

"Whoa, why don't we all just relax here," Pablo interjected. Always trying to be the peacemaker.

"I'm perfectly relaxed," I countered.

"What the fuck is wrong with you, Victor? Ever since Ernie died you've been a complete dick. Hell, even before that."

"Maybe I'm tired of you questioning everything I do."

"*Silencio!*" My father raised his voice.

"Why is everyone yelling?"

All four of us pivoted at the quietly asked question. Estelle stood in the doorway. Her face was ashen, and her gaze darted between all of us before landing on me. I closed the distance between us.

"I'm sorry if we woke you," I murmured softly. I didn't like the fear in her expression.

She stared up at me, her bright blue eyes full of questions. "What's going on, Victor?"

"We're having a family meeting."

"It didn't sound like a very friendly one. Is this about what happened yesterday?"

My thumb brushed her cheek with a gentle sweep. "Why don't you go back upstairs and rest. I'll come up and explain later."

Estelle's expression shifted, and I recognized the stubborn look on her face. She wasn't going to let this go. She

93

straightened to her full height. Which still barely reached my chin.

"I may not be a member of this family, but I think I'm entitled to know what's going on. Especially if it involves me."

"She's right," Manny said.

"Stay out of this," I barked over my shoulder.

"You know what? I'm done here. I don't know what your problem is, but I'm not sticking around for this bullshit."

He snatched up his coat and stormed out the front door slamming it behind him. Both my father and Pablo stared at me with eyes full of disappointment. Without another word, they both walked out of the room, leaving Estelle and me alone. I turned my back on her and paced again. *Why did I let Manuel get on my nerves?*

"You weren't very nice to your brother." she scolded.

Not her too. "I'm tired of his know-it-all attitude."

"What are you talking about?"

Perfect Manuel who never did anything wrong. Him with his perfect wife and two point five kids. Sitting in his house with its white picket fence. Looking down from his pedestal at the rest of us. "Nothing."

"There's obviously something going on between you two. I'm supposed to trust you, yet you won't do the same for me."

Estelle wouldn't understand. "It has nothing to do with trust."

"It does actually."

"Fine. You want to know?"

"I just said I did." She crossed her arms and cocked her hip.

She was infuriating sometimes. "My entire life I've felt

like I'm not good enough. Not smart enough. Ernie, Manny, Pablo—they all dismissed me. Manny was the worst, though. If I had an idea, no matter what it was, he shot it down."

Manny had also turned everything into a contest. It was why I started playing video games after they all moved out. There was no one but me and the game. It didn't become a battle over who was better. I had no one to compete with but myself.

"Did you know I wanted to join the S.W.A.T. team?" I asked, absently.

"No, I didn't know that."

"A couple years ago. I took all the course work. Passed all the field training. Even took the exam." It was the one thing I wanted. I'd worked hard. Studied hard. I was proud of myself. I'd done everything right. Only it wasn't enough.

"What happened?" Estelle's voice was soft.

"There were only two open spots. Some guy I didn't know got one. Manuel got the other."

She laid her hand on my chest. I glanced down at her and winced at the pity in her eyes. I didn't need her to feel sorry for me.

"Have you tried talking to him? Telling him how you feel?"

"Why? It won't do any good. He'll just blow me off. Poor Victor."

"I'm not trying to discount your feelings. I swear. As an outsider who spent a significant amount of time in this house, can I tell you what I experienced whenever I saw you all together?"

I gave a short nod.

"Envy."

She surprised me. That was something I hadn't expected.

"You have no idea how many times I watched the five of you together and wished I had what you had."

My skin burned from the random patterns Estelle drew on my chest. I wanted her to keep touching me. She plucked at my shirt, pulling the fabric and releasing it as she continued.

"There was so much love between you all. I know you guys had disagreements on occasion, but I could see how much you loved each other. Not all of us had that, Victor. I would have traded everything to be part of your family. To have what you and your siblings have."

Her words gutted me. I couldn't imagine what it was like for her growing up.

"At least the five of you had each other. I had no one. Not even parents who loved me."

I couldn't have felt more pain at Estelle's words than if she'd stabbed me.

"You can't keep letting this resentment fester. Eventually the two of you are going to reach the point where your relationship is unsalvageable. I really think you should talk to him. Will it make a difference?" she shrugged. "Who knows. But at least you'll have expressed how you feel. Beyond that, it's up to him."

I pulled her against me, once again needing that connection. Everything was right in my world when I held her close. She fit perfectly in my arms, her soft curves against my hard edges. I never wanted to let her go.

"You're right. I'll talk to them. Even if nothing changes, at least I'll have said my piece."

Her small hands rested against my chest. They were soft and delicate, like her. She was right about the discussion that had to happen. There was one thing she needed to know though. One correction about her life I needed to make, because she had it wrong. I cupped her jaw in both of my palms keeping my eyes locked on hers. I wanted her to see the vow, the promise in them. Her entire body was still. She wasn't even breathing.

"You may not have had anyone in the past, but that's no longer the case. You have me. I'm yours now for however long you keep me."

CHAPTER 15

YOU HAVE ME.

Victor's words kept playing over and over in my head. I missed anything he said after that. Those three words were all my brain homed in on. They sounded far too close to those other three little words.

You have me.

It was terrifying how much I liked hearing them. The intensity behind them was more than I was ready for. It didn't stop me from adding them to the memory box I was building inside my head. I was going to need those reminders. Because I wanted to be able to trust this moment right here. I was *desperate* for it.

"I'm really glad I have you." That was all I could commit to at the moment, but considering my feelings about relationships, that small concession was a giant step for me. "So, why don't you tell me what you were talking about in the meeting."

Victor stepped back with a frustrated sigh. "We were discussing the fact that we still don't have any answers.

There's nothing that ties the attempt to grab you and the crash yesterday together, yet they can't be a coincidence. Not within only a few days of each other. Which means we're back to square one with zilch to go on."

I could understand his discouragement. It was a struggle living with the unknown. "You still think Álvarez could be behind it?"

"My gut keeps saying yes, but the fact is…I don't know. No one's been able to confirm his location. If anyone does know anything, they're not talking. I'm not surprised. He's a highly wanted man after Brody turned over all his evidence. I'm actually surprised they haven't apprehended him in Mexico yet and extradited him back here to stand trial. He must be deep in hiding. "

It was the little things about Victor I was truly starting to notice. Like the fact that not only did he pace when he was frustrated, but he ran his hands through his hair as well. Right now he was almost wearing a path in the carpet, and his hair was mussed. I found it incredibly sexy. The intensity he gave off.

"Brody's brother wants to help see if he can get any information on Álvarez's whereabouts."

That gave me pause. Brody's brother?

"Isn't that dangerous for him given his…circumstances?" I wasn't sure how else to put it. How did one describe a person's drug addiction?

"Probably. We don't have a lot of other options. In fact, we might be reaching, but it would be great if I could just get some confirmation, one way or another, whether Álvarez is hiding in Chicago somewhere. If he is, then at least we have a concrete suspect for both incidents. If he's not, then we chalk up what happened as random. Which doesn't make me happy either."

I knew Victor. Nothing would make him happy until someone was behind bars. If I had a vote, it would be for the attempt to take me as random. Even as horrifying as it was to think that I was just picked off the street to try and grab, it also meant it was safe for me to leave here. I could go home. Back to my own house. Alone. The idea didn't sound as appealing as it had a week ago. Especially now, with this... thing between Victor and me.

"What are you thinking right now?"

"Hmm, what?" His pacing had brought him back to standing right in front of me. I hadn't heard him move.

"You had this look on your face. I was curious what was going on inside that beautiful head of yours."

I wish I could control the flush that crawled up my cheeks every time he looked at me like he was now. Like he had that one day, long ago, outside Ines' room. His focus was entirely on me and his brown eyes darkened with intensity. Every time he looked at me like this, it was like we were the only two people on earth. It made me want to touch him. Everywhere.

"Oh. I was just thinking that if there wasn't more to it, I mean if Álvarez hadn't targeted me, then I guess I wouldn't need to stay here anymore."

From the scowl that crossed Victor's face, he was as happy about the idea as I was. Here we were, talking about kidnappings, car crashes, and the cartel, but that wasn't what was on my mind. It was not being around Victor day in and day out. It was funny how things could change in a single day. Maybe it was the crash. Or maybe it was that kiss. Yesterday morning I'd been so ready to leave. Today, I wasn't so sure. I was so confused. "I guess we'll cross that bridge when we get to it."

In the meantime, I'd stay here, and we'd figure out where he and I went from here.

"I guess so. I'll see what Preston can find about Álvarez. If it's nothing, then I'll take you home. I'd rather not take any chances with your safety."

I was actually relieved that I wasn't going to have to go home quite yet. Spending more time with Victor sounded much better than going back to my empty house.

CHAPTER 16

Estelle was right. I needed to talk to Manuel. He hadn't come by the house this morning. My brother *never* missed coming to breakfast during the week even if he already ate at home with his wife. After a quick glance at the clock, I picked up my phone and dialed.

"Hello?"

"Hey, it's me."

"Yeah." His flat, single word response spoke volumes. I should probably be doing this in person, but this made things easier. For me, at least.

"You got a minute?"

"I suppose."

I bit back the sarcastic retort I wanted to make. This was about getting shit off my chest, not starting another argument.

"From the time I could walk, all I ever wanted was to be like my big brothers. I'd follow the three of you around. Trying to prove that I could do everything you guys did. But no matter what, you always knocked me down. I was never strong enough or smart enough."

"That's not true," Manuel argued.

"It is actually. Maybe you didn't see it, but that's how it was. How it's always been. How it still is. Just like the S.W.A.T. team. It's gotten tiresome after twenty-eight years."

There it was.

"What about the team?" He sounded genuinely confused.

"I applied to join a couple years ago. Got almost perfect scores on all the exams and in field training. Guess who was chosen?"

"Jesus, Victor," Manny breathed out.

"There's been so many things over the years. I've lost count, in fact. Actually, I stopped counting a long time ago."

"I don't even know what to say."

I shrugged although he couldn't see me. "There isn't really anything *to* say."

Now that I'd said it, it was true. I didn't plan on carrying this around any longer. It didn't do me any good holding on to it other than make me bitter towards my brother. Estelle was right. The only thing it would do was put a strain on our family.

"I never realized." I heard Manuel swallow hard. "I'm sorry, Victor."

"I appreciate that. But I didn't tell you to get an apology. It was to let go of the hold it had on me. Well, that's all I wanted to say. Thanks for listening."

"Um, yeah, no problem." His confusion and difficulty with putting words together was almost comical.

I inhaled a huge breath and let it out releasing all the tension inside me. It was actually a relief to have that off my chest. Glad to have gotten that out of the way, I needed to call Preston before Gladstone picked me up for work. My truck was still in the body shop, but I was supposed to have it back in the next few days.

I picked up my phone again.

"Hello?"

"Hey, it's Victor."

"I was actually about to call you."

"What's going on?"

"I have a deal going down tomorrow night."

I sighed. "Look, about that. I don't think it's a great idea for you to put either of us in this position. I'll feel guilty and responsible if shit goes wrong. I thought of another plan."

"What other plan?"

"Álvarez used to own a strip club that dealt drugs in the back room. It's where my sister was undercover, and where she met your brother. I think we should go check it out."

"When?"

"Tonight. After I get off work. I'll come pick you up around midnight, and we can head over there."

Preston was silent. "You think we'll get any info there?"

"I don't know, but it's a place to start. If not, we'll figure it out from there."

"Fine. Pick me up outside of Mickey's at midnight."

"See you then."

The doorbell rang just as I hung up. I grabbed my gun belt off my dresser and bounded down the stairs. My dad let Jonathan in.

"Afternoon, Mr. Rodriguez," he nodded in greeting.

"You know you can call me Ernesto."

"Yes, sir. But my mother raised me to call men I respect mister."

My dad smiled and patted my partner on the cheek. "She raised a good son."

Gladstone glanced over at me. "You ready?"

"Yeah, let me grab my dinner out of the fridge."

I quickly returned with my lunch box and we jumped in the patrol car.

"How's your friend, Estelle, doing? She okay? I heard about the crash from a buddy of mine that works that precinct." Jonathan asked.

"Yeah, she's fine. Thanks for asking."

He waved me off. "No problem, man. I know you care about her. Hopefully we can get a lead on something soon."

"Yeah, me too."

I was quiet the rest of the ride to work. My mind drifted to tonight, and the hope that Preston and I could find something to lead us to Álvarez. I only needed to make it through this shift.

PRESTON and I were sitting in Pablo's car outside *Sweet SINoritas*, the strip club where Ines had gone undercover as a dancer. The clock on my dashboard glowed in the darkness. Heavy tension surrounded us, making the air thick to breathe. I'd parked all the way in the back, in a darkened corner under a broken street light.

"Let me go in first. I was 'Gabriela's' manager. Most likely, word made its way here that she was an undercover cop, so I'm going to have to make sure I can pull off the fact that I had no idea."

Preston shot me a glance. "What if you can't?"

"Then I'm in trouble. Give me ten minutes, then come in.

I'll be in the back corner of the bar. If I'm not there, get out and call the cops."

"I don't know if this is such a good idea."

I reached down and patted my ankle. "I have a weapon, if worse comes to worst."

He scoffed. "A lot of good it will do you if they confiscate it."

"Which is why you're going to call for reinforcements if you don't see me once you get inside."

"Fine. Just be careful."

I nodded and exited the car. A light mist fell and glared off the headlights of passing cars. Puddles formed in the potholes that peppered the gravel parking lot of the club. I stepped over one, the rocks crunching under my soles. My eyes darted along the ground looking for the spot where my sister's blood had pooled after Alejandro had slashed her face all those months ago. I'd never find it though. It had long been washed away. Rage scored my chest at the memory of seeing her the morning after, the stitches bright against her skin. I shook away the imagery and put my game face on. I was about to test my acting skills.

The faint strains of music filtered through the door, growing louder the closer I got. It was a song meant to invoke thoughts of lust and fucking. I swung the door open and was assaulted by a combination of scents. Booze, sweat, perfume, smoke, and sex. Through the smoky interior, the stage was lit up like a bonfire. Bright lights shone down on the topless woman spinning around the metal pole center stage. Her body gyrated, swayed, and moved to the music blasting from the speakers. Her movements were sensual and meant to seduce.

She was pretty, in an exaggerated way, but my eyes

didn't linger. Instead, my gaze drifted around the place. Few tables were occupied, mostly by gray-haired gentleman wearing expensive suits and smoking even more expensive cigars. The DJ in the corner wore headphones and was staring down at his equipment, most likely queuing up the next song.

I headed toward the bar, keeping alert to any noise or unexpected movement from the few occupants. I moved all the way to the end of the bar and slid onto a stool with my back to the wall behind me. The bartender, Damon, approached.

Time to put my game face on.

"Luis, long time no see," he greeted while wiping out a glass with a towel.

I pasted on a smile and reached out to shake his hand. "What has it been? Seven, eight months?"

His gaze flicked to my outstretched hand before he threw the towel over his shoulder and reluctantly accepted the gesture.

"What are you doing here?" His eyes narrowed in suspicion.

I pointed in the direction of the stage. "Looking for some fresh talent. There's a huge pole dancing competition happening at this club downtown in a couple months. The purse is ten Gs. I thought I'd see if you had any prospects around here."

"What about your one chick? Gabriela was her name, I believe." Damon emphasized her name with sarcasm and air quotes.

Shit. I guess that answered that question. I drew back in confusion. "Yeah, Gabby. What's with the weirdness, man?"

He stared me down, but I kept the confused expression on my face. "You don't know?"

I held my hands up. "The only thing I know is about six months ago she stopped returning my calls. I dropped by her apartment, but her landlord said she'd up and left him high and dry. Hadn't paid rent in two months. Hell"—I shrugged, almost abashed—"I even went to the cops and reported her missing, but of course, they blew me off. No one gives a shit about some stripper."

Damon leaned in, his eyes darting around the room checking for prying ears, before stage-whispering. "Man, she wasn't a stripper. She was an undercover cop."

I reared back in disbelief. "Are you serious?"

He leaned back with arms raised in surrender. "Swear to god. Alejandro showed up here one night after hours and sliced her face all to hell. A couple days after that, rumors started flying. Alejandro was dead. She was a cop. One of Álvarez's top dogs was in the D.E.A.. It was some crazy shit, man."

I let a rush of air escape. "Damn. Didn't Mr. Álvarez own this club?"

Damon shook his head. "Man, do you live under a rock or something? He was the head of the fucking cartel. After all that shit went down, the cops raided everything he owned. According to the news, he escaped back to Mexico and is hiding out."

"How is this place still in business then?"

He straightened proudly. "After a while, it went up for auction, and I bought it. Cleaned it up a little. Called some of the girls and offered them their jobs back. This is a lucrative business. Not as much as when Álvarez owned it, but it still draws in the cash."

"Wow, I'm impressed. I remember there were a couple of good dancers when I was here last. Maybe one of them will be interested in my offer."

Movement caught my eye. Preston was making his way across the floor. I waved him over, signaling the all clear. I clasped his hand and pulled him in for a single shoulder bump and pulled back.

"Hey man, glad you could make it. Damon, this is my buddy, Preston."

The both jerked their chins upward in the universal male gesture for "what's up?".

"Pleasure. Let me grab you guys a couple beers. Feel free to chat with any of the ladies. I know a couple who could really use the extra cash."

"Thanks."

He disappeared. I swiveled in my seat toward Preston, my gaze traveling over his shoulder to stare out at the place. Even if Damon was the new owner, it was possible some previous regulars might have some information on Álvarez's whereabouts.

"Everything going okay?"

"Yeah, we're good. The place recently came under new ownership, but most, if not all, of the same ladies work here. That's about all I got so far. Bartender bought the place. Said he cleaned it up. Not sure what his idea of that is."

Out of the corner of my eye, I caught movement. A young woman wearing a bright red silk robe tied at the waist headed in our direction. Shit. I'd completely forgotten about Michele. I didn't know much about her other than she was a nineteen-year-old single mother paying her way through college. She'd been friends with "Gabriela", although Ines told me before she and Brody left that

Michele knew the truth about them. I hope she'd kept their secret.

"Hey"—she cast a quick glance in Preston's direction —"Luis."

Her caution with using that name told me everything I needed to know. "Michele. How've you been?"

"Good. Only about two semesters left of school."

"Congratulations. This is my friend, Preston. He knows a couple of our mutual friends."

Despite being half-naked, face plastered with makeup, and thigh high boots on, she didn't flirt. "Hi."

Preston nodded. "Nice to meet you."

Damon reappeared with our beers.

"Here you go, gentleman."

Preston turned his attention to the beer that was set in front of him, picking at the label with his finger.

"Michele, you're up in two sets."

She nodded at the reminder. "I'll be ready."

The three of us were left alone again. She leaned in slightly. "How is she? Are they okay?"

"Everything's fine. Well, with them anyway," I assured her.

Michele sagged in relief. "I'm glad. It's been a few months since we talked. She said it wasn't safe anymore. Told me she couldn't call me again. I've been worried sick."

Guilt flooded me. Ines had asked me to let the girl know she was okay, but after this place shut down, I let it go. I should have taken the time to find her. "I'm sorry. We do have another problem though."

"Anything I can help with?"

It wasn't safe to drag this poor girl into this. I shook my head.

"No, but thanks anyway."

A song began and Michele swiveled her head toward the DJ. She pivoted back. "Shit. I'm up. Please don't leave before I'm done."

She hurried to the back of the stage to get ready for her set while I turned back to Preston. "I'm glad you're not dragging her into this. It's too dangerous. It may not have even been a great idea to talk to her," he said.

I snuck a peek at the room. No one seemed to be paying us any attention. Preston was right, though. If I'd known she was here —. It was too late now, though. The best thing we could do was not come back. Based on the current clientele, we probably weren't going to get any information from anyone anyway.

"You're right. We'll have to come up with another plan. Keep her, and any of the other women, out of this. If anyone here *is* still in contact with Álvarez, word could get back to him. I've already got one woman I need to protect. I don't need another."

I passed when Damon offered to bring us another beer. Preston hadn't drunk a drop of his first one. Michele finished her dance and hurried back over.

At her approach, we both stood. "We're going to get going, but it was good to see you. I'll tell our friend you asked about her. We won't be back here. It's not safe. If you ever need anything, though, go to the station house over on Walton and ask for me or my father."

Michele nodded solemnly. "I understand. Thank you for letting me know she's okay. I miss her."

She gave me a quick hug before disappearing toward the dressing rooms.

CHAPTER 17

THE KNOCK on my bedroom door startled me. I was surprised to see Ernesto on the other side holding the cordless phone. I'd been expecting Victor. Considering his flat expression, I wished it was. Whoever was on the other line wasn't someone I cared to speak to.

"For you, *mi burbujita*. Your father."

Annnnd, he was right. Dread spread through me. It had been almost a week since Pauline had called with her drunken ramblings. To be honest, I was surprised this was the first call from George. Usually Pauline lorded over him all her useless knowledge, because she knew it would piss him off. My staying at the Rodriguez house was sure to have done that. Anger at my time spent here had been the only thing my parents had ever agreed upon. My father had never forgotten about one long ago night in particular and made sure to mention it any time I saw or talked to him. Ernesto was probably his least favorite person.

Sensing Victor's father's concern, I gave him my best, albeit forced, smile and took the phone.

"I'll be downstairs if you need me," he said, kindly.

While I appreciated everything he'd ever done for me, I'd learned long ago how to handle George.

"Thank you."

Like ripping off a bandage, I needed to get this over with. Who knew how long afterward I'd have to hide in my room. I was never good company after a phone call, or rare dinner, with either of my parents.

"Hello, George."

His heave of disgust didn't surprise me. "Such disrespect. I shouldn't be surprised. You are your mother's daughter after all. How many children call their fathers by their first name? None that I know of. I don't understand why you insist on being so difficult, Estelle."

My fingers ached from the tight grip I maintained on the phone. I had to forcibly unclench them when all I wanted to do was keep squeezing until I crushed the receiver into a pile of dust.

"Did you need something?"

"I understand you're staying with that family again. *Without* Ines being there. What purpose does that serve? You're a grown up now, Estelle. There's no reason for you to run to them all the time."

Not once did George ever take responsibility for his part in why I ran to Ines' house. To this day, it baffled me that he hadn't ever taken a step back and realized that it was his and my mother's volatile relationship that pushed me here. This house was safe.

"If you only called to insult my friend's family, then our conversation is over."

My threat worked, because George's sigh was filled with defeat. "I called because your birthday is coming up in a few days, and since I'll be away at work, I'd like to take you out to dinner tonight."

He had me utterly flabbergasted.

"I don't think I'm going to be able to make it," I hedged.

"It's your thirtieth birthday. It's an important milestone. One we need to celebrate."

For a brief moment, I didn't know if I wanted to laugh or cry.

"Why are you laughing? Estelle?"

Tears of mirth trailed down my cheeks. I couldn't catch my breath. With gasps of choked back laughter, I managed to form words. "I'm… only…twenty… seven."

"I'm sorry, what? I didn't understand you."

Wiping away tears, I chortled a few times, and inhaled a hiccuped breath. "I said"—shaky chuckle—"I'm twenty-seven. Not thirty."

There was silence on the other end. I hoped my father was drowning in his idiocy. He finally cleared his throat and continued as though my revelation was of no concern. "I've made us a reservation for seven o'clock at *Spiaggia*."

It was like speaking to a brick wall. "Did you not hear what I said? Tonight isn't a good night." Tomorrow wouldn't be any better. Or the next night. Most likely not the next either.

"Why don't you bring that Victor boy with you?"

This entire conversation made my blood pressure rise. I needed to get off the phone. Now. "Fine. I'll talk to him and get back to you."

It filled me with immense pleasure to hang up, cutting off George mid-sentence. A growl of frustration rose out of my chest. I barely restrained myself from screaming and throwing the phone across the room.

"Estelle? You okay?" There was a soft knock behind Victor's muffled words. The hinges creaked when he cracked open the door and hesitantly stuck his head in. "I was actually on my way to come find you when my dad said your father was on the phone. I wanted to make sure you were all right."

It was sweet that he came to check on me. It was also not…great. My anger level was still at the top of the thermometer and ready to explode out of it. I could see shattering glass spraying everyone with the vitriol I wanted to scream.

"Not really." It had been a long time since I'd cried tears of rage, but I was on the edge. I hated that my father had reduced me to this. He didn't even care either. That's what made it that much worse. No, actually what made it worse, was that I continued to let him.

Victor stepped through the door and closed it behind him. "What can I do to help?"

For all his flippant ways, he knew when it was time to step up. I wasn't used to offers of help from anyone, so my first instinct was to say nothing. It was often easier that way. No expectations to be upheld. I was trying to change though. Rely on someone, Victor, more.

"Apparently George made dinner reservations for him and me tonight to celebrate my thirtieth birthday, and as usual, didn't listen when I told him it wasn't a good time."

Victor's face crinkled in confusion. "Your what birthday?"

My laugh was humorless. "That's pretty much what I said."

He was actually at a loss for words for a minute. "I'm not even going to try and puzzle that one out."

"You're better off not."

"You know, I could always go with you if you'd like."

My heart pitter-pattered at his offer. "Funny you should mention that. He suggested I bring 'that Victor boy'. Before I hung up on him, I said I'd ask, but mostly to placate him."

Victor pulled me into his arms. His heat seeped through his t-shirt and straight into me to push away the cold I hadn't known I was feeling. I nearly purred when he petted my hair. It soothed some of my hostility for which I was grateful.

"One day you'll believe me when I tell you, you only have to ask for my help. It's free for the offering. No matter what. No matter when. Without stipulations or conditions."

Everything in me was desperate to believe him. I snuggled closer, the feel of soft cotton against my skin, the scent of fabric softener, and Victor finally washing away the last remnants of anger that had lingered.

"Thank you. Are you sure you don't mind coming with me?" I murmured against his chest, his heart beat strong in my ear. His arms tightened around me in a protective gesture against any harm that threatened me.

"Not at all. Where are we going, and what time are we supposed to be there?"

"Reservations are for seven at *Spiaggia*."

Victor whistled. "Fancy. So, we'll be there at ten after?" Amusement colored his question.

I pulled back to look up at him with a raised brow. There was a twinkle in his eye. "You don't think showing up ten minutes late is childish? I thought about it but didn't want to appear petty. Also, I know George. I'm not inclined to sit there from the time we're seated until our order is taken or

LK SHAW

beyond listening to him lecture me about common courtesy and timeliness."

His eyes widened. "He'd really do that?"

"My father does nothing but criticize or complain about everything I do or say. He isn't happy unless he makes everyone else around him miserable. Of course, his own miserableness is never his fault. Someone else is always to blame."

Victor palmed my jaw with his calloused hand. I leaned into his touch, loving the feel of his rough skin against my cheek. It was the hand of someone who worked hard. A shiver skittered down my spine at the thought of his rough hands touching me everywhere.

"He sounds extremely unpleasant." His expression tightened, and his mouth flattened.

"It won't be a fun evening, that's for sure. In fact, I'd be more than happy not to go, but…" my voice trailed off, not really wanting to explain it.

Victor nodded solemnly. "It's easier to just go along with things and get them over with as peaceably and quickly as possible. It's a few hours of discomfort compared to days or weeks of continuous berating and guilt trips through phone calls."

I couldn't believe he'd actually understood without me having to explain it. No one ever really *got* it before. "Exactly."

"I'll try and deflect as much of the criticism as possible. Maybe we'll get lucky, and he'll direct it all toward me. I don't know him, but I have no invested interest in his feelings about me, so nothing he says will bother me. Besides, if he gets too obnoxious, we'll leave."

Unknown feelings rushed through me. I raised up and

kissed him, trying to convey all my words in the touch of my lips against his.

"Thank you." I whispered against his mouth.

"You're welcome. Why don't you call him back and let him know we'll see him tonight."

We broke apart and Victor left me in my room to make my phone call. Tonight suddenly didn't seem like it would be the usual nightmare.

CHAPTER 18

How could a father treat his child the way it seemed like he'd treated her? It only reinforced my need to protect her. Let him say what he wanted about me, but he'd watch his mouth when it came to her.

A glance at the clock said it was time to go. I'd only been half-joking about showing up late. Yes, it was passive aggressive, but at the same time it would give me a tiny sense of satisfaction to make him wait for us. It would only add fuel to the fire though, and that was the last thing I wanted for Estelle.

I stood outside her room, my palms sweating like a teenager's on prom night. She opened the door and all the blood shot straight to my cock. Estelle had curled her hair so it settled in waves over her shoulders and fanned around her perfect breasts. Her lips were cherry red. The color made me want to taste them and see if they were as sweet as they looked. Her blue eyes were big and bold and made her entire face that much more beautiful. She looked gorgeous.

Pink darted across her cheeks. "You're staring."

I blinked and cleared my throat. I desperately needed to adjust my straining cock but didn't want to draw attention to the hard-on she'd given me. "Sorry. You look great."

"Thank you." Her smile was electric.

I needed to feel her touch, so I held out my arm. "You ready?"

Estelle slipped her arm through mine. "Not even close to it." Nervousness coated her words.

I squeezed her hand in reassurance before we headed downstairs. "It'll be fine. We'll eat, drink a glass of wine, small talk for a bit, and then we'll leave. Two hours, tops."

I opened the car door for her, and she settled onto the gray leather seat. She stared up at me. "You have a lot more faith than I do. I really hope you're right."

"I am. You'll see," I reassured her, closing the door while she buckled her seatbelt.

Before long we were downtown. My eyes scanned both sides of the parking garage trying to find a parking spot. Nothing. I had no idea it would be this busy on a weeknight.

"Damn it," I cursed.

"There," Estelle pointed at the white reverse lights that glowed from a car three spaces away from us. I waited for the vehicle to pull out and then pulled in. The night hadn't really started and I was already annoyed. It didn't bode well for how the rest of the evening could go.

We walked hand-in-hand toward the restaurant. The night was chilly, but there were still a few people strolling the sidewalks despite it being twilight. Signs of fall and Halloween, from pumpkins to skeletons, were displayed in the brightly lit storefront windows we passed before reaching the restaurant door. Estelle stopped before we could enter. Her fingers tightened on mine.

"It's going to be fine, remember?" I sent her a reassuring smile and rubbed my thumb across hers to try and soothe her. She returned my smile with a shaky one of her own.

"Good evening. How many?" The hostess greeted us, her voice barely carrying over the din of conversation and clatter from the kitchen. The prevalent scent of yeast rolls and garlic made my mouth water.

"We're with the Jenkins party." Estelle's voice was strong and confident despite her earlier signs of trepidation.

The hostess glanced down at her podium and grabbed a couple menus. "Right this way, please."

I followed the two women, making eye contact with everyone who glanced in my direction. Even off duty, I was always a cop. It was important to be aware of my surroundings. The restaurant was busy with almost every table and booth we passed filled. The hostess stopped in front of a four-seat, square table in the middle of the dining area. Her father sat alone, arms folded in front of him.

"George," she greeted.

"Have a seat." He didn't smile. Nothing but the simple order.

I pulled out Estelle's chair and sat next to her. I glanced over and met the same cobalt blue eyes I saw every time I looked at Estelle. So, this was her father.

The hostess laid our menus down. "Your server will be right with you." She smiled pleasantly before disappearing.

Her father scowled. "You're late." That was it. Just those two words.

Under the table, she reached out to squeeze my hand. She clutched it so tightly, I could feel her nails digging in. Most likely leaving crescent shaped indentations in my flesh.

"It was my fault, sir." I reached my free hand out for a

conciliatory shake. "Victor Rodriguez. A pleasure to finally meet you."

Now that I had his full attention, his eyes scanned over me. His handshake was quick and perfunctory. His top lip twitched, almost moving into a snarl. I read the disdain in his expression. I wasn't bothered by it. So long as he continued directing it toward me and not Estelle.

"A pleasure." It clearly was not.

Our waitress arrived at our table and took our drink orders before rushing off to fill them.

"So, Victor, I understand you're a police officer."

"Yes, sir. Seven years now." We were a family of officers dating back to my great-grandfather, who'd emigrated here from Mexico when he was only a boy. I was proud of my family lineage and the path we'd taken.

"Must be a difficult job riding around in a car all day."

Estelle bristled next to me. It was obvious he was trying to get a rise out of me. It didn't work. "Yes, sir, it sure is. It does get a little easier when someone tries to shoot and kill us though."

Jackass. Beside me Estelle coughed to hide her laugh while I stared stony-eyed at her father. He stared back, but I didn't give an inch. A measure of triumph blasted through me as his gaze darted away from mine. He cleared his throat. His attention turned back to Estelle.

"I suppose you're still teaching at that little elementary school." His tone was condescending. "I thought you were going back to graduate school for your doctorate and becoming a college professor?

"That might have been something I'd thought about three years ago. Briefly. It definitely hasn't been on my radar in any way since then."

I didn't think Estelle could squeeze my hand harder, but she proved me wrong. All my fingers were numb at this point.

"You could be doing so much more with your life, Estelle. Being a babysitter for someone else's children is hardly something you should be striving for."

"Estelle is hardly a babysitter. She's a highly qualified teacher providing a quality education. What she does is important. I'm sure I would have turned out a lot smarter if I'd had someone of her caliber guiding me through school." I turned my head to face her before continuing. "Her students are lucky to have someone as kind and compassionate as Estelle."

I made eye contact with her father to drive my next point home. "If only more people were like her."

Fuck this guy. I didn't know if I was making things better or worse. Estelle was perfectly capable of speaking for herself, but I couldn't sit here and listen to him disparage the job she did. One she loved. I didn't care if he was her father.

"I *knew* that was you over here." The proclamation was high pitched and slurred. We all turned at the interruption, including those at the tables nearest us, to see a blonde woman in black heels and a red dress stumbling in our direction. She carried a rocks glass in the hand she was using to point angrily at us, amber liquid spilling over the top of it

"Are you fucking kidding me?" Estelle murmured behind me.

The woman drew closer, her lipstick partially smeared, and sneered. "You can have dinner with your *father*, but you can't even be bothered to call me, your own mother?"

Jesus, it was a damn family reunion. Not a pleasant one at that. Now that she was right on us, I could see the vague resemblance between her and Estelle. Only the years hadn't been kind to the former Mrs. Jenkins. Dark circles were under her eyes and her skin had the tanned, leathery appearance of someone who spent far too much time in the sun or a tanning bed.

"Fancy meeting you here, Pauline." The smug tone coloring Mr. Jenkins' words caused me to turn. He didn't seem all that surprised to see the woman here. I cast a quick glance in Estelle's direction. Her expression could have been carved from stone. In fact, she didn't even appear to be breathing.

"You know this is my favorite restaurant, asshole." Pauline jabbed her glass in the direction of her ex-husband, more liquid spilling over the top to splash across our table. My eyes watered from the scent of liquor oozing out of her pores. She smelled like a distillery.

George smirked and tried to appear innocent. "How was I supposed to know you still came here? It's not as those I keep track of your whereabouts."

By now, we were the center of attention. People at nearby tables were whispering to each other and not so discreetly pointing. Another glance at Estelle told me she was barely holding it together. She was staring at her father with horror. Her entire body was rigid and her fingers were white from clutching them tightly in her lap. *When had she let go of my hand?*

"Did you know she was going to be here? Is that why you invited me?" The words escaped her clenched jaw. They were filled with pain she couldn't disguise.

Her mom spun, and she drunkenly blinked down at us. "I can't believe how ungrateful you are."

My head snapped in Pauline's direction. "Don't speak to her like that."

Her eyes flashed with hatred. "You're that Rodriguez boy, aren't you? The one Estelle's been panting after since she was a teenager?"

There was a choked sob at my left.

That was it. We were done here.

I jerked my chair back and stood towering over Pauline, and George, who'd remained sitting. Judging by his smirk, he was enjoying the show. Neither of them were worth my time. I reached for the only person I cared about in this entire thing.

"You ready to get out of here?"

Estelle jumped to her feet and took off. I followed right behind her.

"Where are—"

"Selfish—"

I whirled on her parents, the rage burning a fire through my veins. "Both of you need to shut your mouths," I hissed. "I don't know who the fuck you think you are, but neither of you are fit to call yourselves parents."

Not even waiting for a reply, I spun around. Estelle was gone. *Fuck*. I raced to the front door and outside. Panic set in when I didn't see her.

"Estelle?" I yelled.

I twirled a one-eighty, my heart in my throat. A shadow shifted near the building. She stepped out from her hiding spot. I sagged in relief and breathed out her name on a whisper. Her face was awash with tears that sparkled under the street lighting shining down on her. Slowly, I approached like she was a wounded animal ready to spook at the slightest movement. I stopped toe to toe with her. I reached up to wipe the wetness off her red, cold cheeks.

She flinched and avoided my gaze. "Take me home. Please." Her voice cracked on the last.

"Este—"

"Now," she barked out.

Goddamn her parents. I nodded. "Okay."

I tried holding her hand, but she jerked it away. Her stride was rigid like a soldier marching in formation. The ride home was tense and silent. I wanted to talk about this but didn't want to push. Not after what just went down back there. I'd give her time to cool off. Tomorrow was soon enough to discuss this.

Estelle dove out of the car the minute I shifted into park. Dread was heavy inside me. Tonight wasn't supposed to go like this. She was hurting. I felt helpless, because she wouldn't let me try and ease her pain. Instead she was shutting me out.

"You two are home…" My father's voice trailed off when he spotted us. I shook my head.

What scared me the most was how quietly she closed the bedroom door behind her. I knocked, but she didn't open it.

"Fuck," I cursed under my breath. Torn with indecision, I stood outside her room for another minute. She wasn't going to come out.

I pressed my cheek against the wood, desperate to get through to her. "We need to talk. I'll be here when you're ready."

CHAPTER 19

I'D BEEN STARING, dry and gritty-eyed, at the cork board that decorated Ines' bedroom wall for the past thirty minutes. Pictures of the two of us from kindergarten through college decorated it. My eyes landed on one photo in particular. It was one of Ines and me, but standing on my other side was Victor. The three of us were in our bathing suits, soaking wet, on the beach in front of the lake. The sky was the perfect shade of blue with not a cloud in sight. The sun shone so bright the water behind us sparkled like a million diamonds.

We had our arms thrown over each other's shoulders, and we were all laughing. Like the full on belly laugh that ends with tears flowing down your cheeks. Ines and I couldn't have been more than nine, which would have put Victor around eleven. It was so long ago, I couldn't even remember what made us laugh that hard. But I remember everything else about that day. It was the one where my parents told me they were getting divorced. Or rather Pauline screamed at George that she was divorcing him, threw several vases across the room, and then stormed out of the house, most likely to head to the closest bar. That was the day I stopped believing in love.

Dinner had been an epic clusterfuck. I didn't think my parents could hurt me any more than they already had, but tonight showed me otherwise. I was used to being their pawn. Their way to punish the other. But for Victor to witness it? It had been too much. I couldn't do it anymore. It was time to end it.

Decision made, I crawled out of bed and headed down the hall. I didn't hesitate this time. My knock on Victor's door sounded loud in the quiet of the night. It only took seconds before the barrier between us opened. I hurtled past him, not waiting for an invitation.

"I'm done."

"Estelle—"

"No!" I whipped around to face him. "Let me finish."

I needed to get this all out before I lost my courage.

He stood rigidly. "Fine."

"For twenty-seven years I've lived with two people who made each other miserable. I couldn't tell you when they started hating one another. Did it happen right after the wedding? Maybe right after I was born? I don't know. But their hatred is all I've ever known. I don't have any memories of being happy with them."

That was the one thing that had stuck out at me while I'd stared at the cork board of pictures. In every photo, I was happy. Being around this family made me happy. They made me feel loved.

"I knew, I *knew* tonight was going to be awful, but I agreed to go anyway. Do you know why?"

"No." Victor filled the silence.

"Because no matter how many times they use me, no matter how many times they hurt me, there's still that tiny part that thinks maybe this time will be different. Maybe this time it isn't about their hate for the other. For once in their fucking lives, maybe they've started to love me." My voice cracked, but I didn't break.

"Estelle," Victor whispered, wrapping his arms around me. I didn't fight it. Instead, I clutched him tight.

"They don't love me. I don't even think they love themselves."

Victor was quiet. What could he say?

"It's time to accept that nothing is going to change. So, I'm done. Completely and utterly. There aren't going to be any more dinners. If either of them call, I won't answer. If either drops by my house unexpectedly, I'm not home. I don't need the constant reminder of their hatred in my life."

I needed to look him in the eyes no matter how hard this was for me to say. Mostly because I was terrified. But I wanted to re-capture that feeling from those photos. I wanted to be happy. To be loved. Victor released me when I pulled away. I didn't go far. The heat of his body still penetrated mine. His musky scent surrounded me. I tipped my head back to meet his gaze.

"I'm done pushing you away. I want us to work. It's not going to be easy for me, but I'm prepared to fight for you. Even if it's myself I'm fighting against. I care about you, and I really want to believe in love. I'm not saying we're going to fall in love with each other, but I'm hoping you can teach me that it could be possible."

I leaned into Victor's caress. His hand was strong and warm against my cheek. My eyelids fluttered close. The touch of his lips feathered across mine before he deepened the kiss. I opened for him, and he swept his tongue inside. It was a kiss full of unspoken promises, but I could taste each one.

"It's definitely possible," he murmured against my lips. "More than possible actually."

A kernel of hope grew in my chest. One I wanted to nurture. I breathed in his scent, getting drunk on the aroma. My body cried out for more. I slid my hands under his shirt to feel his skin against mine. Victor groaned against my mouth and his kiss turned more ferocious. I sucked in a breath at the tightening of his grip against my hips, pulling me roughly against him. His erection was hard against my belly.

I lost track of all space and time until the back of my knees hit the bed, and I toppled backwards with Victor following me. A rush of air escaped, but he swallowed it down. I couldn't get enough of touching him. I needed more. Tugging on his shirt, I slid it up and he broke our kiss only long enough for me to slip it over his head and toss it to the side. Then he was back, biting and nibbling at my mouth.

My legs separated and Victor settled himself between my thighs rocking his pelvis against me and generating a heated friction. I dug my heels into his ass and ground myself up against him desperate for release. I blinked up at the pitch-black eyes that stared down at me. His arms caged my head, and he brushed my hair off my face.

"You're so fucking beautiful. I remember it hitting me. You were sixteen. I looked at you, and the entire world spun off its axis. I'd seen you day in and day out for years, but on that afternoon your radiance couldn't be denied any longer. You knocked me off my feet, and I've never been the same since."

Victor's words settled over me like a warm, soft blanket. With us lying here like this, I felt beautiful. And powerful. I played with the ridges and valleys of his back, memorizing the feel of each muscle beneath my fingertips. The way they flexed and danced.

"Kiss me again."

He didn't waste a single second. Victor crashed his lips against mine and the fuse was lit. The only way tonight was going to end was with an explosion. I couldn't wait to go up in flames. He pulled my shirt up and we separated only long enough for it to go over my head. Then he took my mouth again. Our hands couldn't move fast enough. Clothing flew off until finally we were nothing but heated flesh against heated flesh.

Our sweat-slicked skin glided against each other. Victor's mouth covered my breast, engulfing it with hot wetness. His hair was soft between my fingers as I pulled him closer. Lips trailed a path across my chest, and he paid homage to my other breast, showing it the same loving treatment he had the other. I wanted to touch him everywhere, but he had other plans.

Our eyes locked as he kissed his way down my body. My body trembled with each touch of his lips across my lower belly, close to where I needed him the most, but not close enough. I needed more. He knew it, because he merely smiled and nibbled every inch of my inner thighs from one to the other, but skipping over the center.

"Please," I choked out. Sparks from the fuse danced just on the edge of dynamite.

"Please, what?" Victor's breath whispered across my pussy. He only needed to lower his head a fraction of an inch, but instead, he waited for my answer. Torturing me as the ache inside me grew.

"I'm so close. Touch me. Kiss me. Make me explode."

And he did. He devoured me. Lapped up the wetness that soaked me. His tongue dipped inside, drawing more liquid from my body. His teeth latched onto my clit, and I saw stars while he nibbled on the swollen nub, then soothed the sting with his tongue. Victor savored me like I was his favorite dessert.

The spark he'd ignited reached its destination, and the sonic boom of my orgasm ricocheted from my body. Spasms of pleasure ripped through me, obliterating me entirely.

CHAPTER 20

I COULDN'T STOP STARING at the woman wrapped in my arms. Watching Estelle coming apart last night had been more than I'd ever dreamed. My cock twitched in remembrance of the way her mouth had closed over it. She'd wanted to return the favor. I'd come harder than I ever had before. Then she'd fallen asleep curled against my chest.

Blaring music echoed around the room. I untangled her limbs from around me and grabbed my phone off the nightstand. I shut it off and turned back around to face her. Blonde hair was mussed and tangled around her face. She had a red pillow crease line across her cheek. Neither of those mattered. She was still beautiful.

"Morning."

"Hey." Her voice was husky with sleep. I could wake up like this every morning for the rest of my life and I'd be happy. The sheet Estelle was using to try and keep herself covered dipped. She snatched it back up, but I'd still caught a flash of pink nipple. It was the color of cotton candy and just as sweet. My cock twitched.

"I should probably go back to my room. I need to get ready for work."

It bothered me that she wouldn't look me in the eye. I palmed her cheek and gently turned her head toward me. "Talk to me. What's going on inside that head of yours? Are you having regrets this morning?"

My gut clenched at the thought. I really thought we'd reached a turning point last night. Was Estelle having second thoughts now that reality had shown up?

"No, I don't regret it at all."

I sagged in relief. That was all I cared about. The rest we could work out. "So, why won't you look at me?"

Her lids closed for a flash before her gaze locked on mine again. "I've just never woken up in bed with a man before. They always left before morning. It was…weird. Not in a bad way. Just different. I wasn't sure how to act."

Red flashed behind my eyes at the thought of any man in Estelle's bed. Touching her. Kissing her. Inside her. She was mine. No one else was going to touch her. Ever. She'd figure it out soon enough.

"This is me. You don't ever have to be anyone but yourself. It doesn't matter if you're knocking me down a few pegs with your strength and attitude or I'm balls deep inside you."

Her entire chest and face flushed. Still, she smiled. "Wow, you sure know how to romance a lady."

I shot her my cheekiest grin. "I do my best work naked."

Her gaze traveled down my body. The sheet covering my lower half shifted. Her eyes met mine again. "That you do."

Needing to taste her one more time, I grasped her neck and pulled her to me. My mouth fastened to hers and we kissed until both of us were breathless. I dropped a final peck on her lips before patting her hip.

"Come on, we got to get up and get you to work."

Without regard to my nakedness, I climbed out of bed. I heard her moving around while I grabbed clean clothes from my closet and slid on a pair of boxer briefs. I happened a glance over my shoulder and chuckled at her gathering up the clothes I tore off her last night with her naked body wrapped in a sheet. Apparently, Bubbles was modest. It was cute. With her clothes in her arms, I walked her to the door planting one more kiss before opening it. Neither of us had taken two steps before coming to an abrupt halt.

"Oh god," Estelle choked out on a whisper.

"*Buenos días,* Victor. Estelle." My father focused everywhere but on the half-naked woman next to me. "I was just coming up to make sure you were okay after last night. You came home distressed and didn't eat dinner. I made you breakfast whenever you're ready."

He quickly pivoted and bolted back down the stairs. His expression was best described as horrified. I couldn't help laughing, because Estelle's matched his perfectly.

"Stop laughing, asshole. I'm not going downstairs ever again. I'm locking myself in Ines' room and never coming out. How am I expected to ever look at Ernesto again?"

I swiped a tear from my eye. "You should have seen both of your faces."

My arm stung where she slapped me. I rubbed the pain out as she huffed and strode angrily away. The fact that her ass was on full display where the sheet gaped open in the back was one I kept to myself. She wouldn't appreciate the humor. Which was confirmed by the door slamming behind her. I loved her fire. My mind stuttered over the L-word.

Tabling the thought, I quickly washed up in the bathroom before throwing on my clothes and heading downstairs. It was going to be fun to watch my dad squirm when Estelle walked in. He wasn't necessarily old fashioned, but he preferred to not know about his children's sex lives.

"Morning, *papá*."

His eyes darted to the empty space behind me. He let down his guard. "Estelle is still upstairs?"

My stomach rumbled at the sight of the food I piled on my plate. "Yes, sir. She's getting ready for work. I'm not sure if she'll be down to eat. My guess is she's going to hightail it straight out to the car when it's time to leave."

"If I had known where Estelle spent the night, I most definitely would not have stepped foot upstairs. I'm sorry I embarrassed her."

The whole episode was a new experience for us all. He'd never caught a woman leaving my room before. I wasn't sure if the awkwardness was in general or if it was because it was Estelle specifically. Either way, eventually it would all smooth over.

"I'll talk to her. We'll all just ignore it and never speak of it again."

He nodded. "That's probably for the best."

It didn't surprise me to see Estelle come into the kitchen no matter how much she protested she wouldn't. Her courage knew no limits. She straightened her spine and pasted a smile on her face.

"Good morning."

She made straight for the plates and fixed herself one.

"Morning, *mi burbujita*."

Estelle relaxed at the nickname. Her fingertips loosened their grip on the plate she carried. Based on how hard she'd been clutching it, I was surprised it hadn't shattered. Her stride slowed as she walked to the table to sit down. She should have known that nothing could make my father treat her any differently than he always had. He loved her like his own daughter.

Once we'd all finished eating, we followed our same routine. I gave her a ride to work and then spent the entire day thinking about her until it was time to pick her up again.

CHAPTER 21

"HAPPY BIRTHDAY, BEAUTIFUL."

The kiss to the nape of my neck startled me for a second before I leaned back into Victor's embrace. The feelings this man gave me. They were like nothing else. He made me feel protected. Safe. Cherished. Like we could conquer the world together. Then my brain processed his words. I spun in his arms. "Wait, how'd you know it was today?"

The dinner from hell was supposed to have allegedly celebrated it, but I had no idea Victor knew the exact date. He pulled me close, and his musky scent enveloped us.

"I'll admit I cheated and pulled up your information at work."

I should be pissed, or at least weirded out, that he used his position with the police to look me up. Instead warmth spread through me that he actually cared enough to find out in order to make me feel special. Another crack began in the wall I'd built around my heart. Each day that passed only further deconstructed this belief system I'd been hanging on to the last eighteen years. The one that said love only caused

141

pain and heartache. Love only lead people down a path of destruction.

With each gesture, Victor was forging a new path for me to travel. I was still treading lightly in this unknown territory. Every day though, my footsteps grew more confident in the direction they were taking me. I could only continue moving forward, hoping I wasn't led astray.

"Well, I don't care how you found out. Thank you for the happy birthday."

"You're welcome." Victor nuzzled my nose and kissed my forehead. "I've been thinking. Yeah, I know, don't hurt—"

I pressed my finger over his lips to stop the flow of words. "Think all you want. Cause I'm really starting to like the way you do it."

Victor kissed the tip of my finger before I pulled it back. "As I was saying, I've been thinking about what to do for your birthday."

"Oh, you don't have to do anything."

I didn't think it was possible, but he pulled me even more flush against him.

"I know I don't have to. I want to. Now stop interrupting me." He softened the command with a smile. "It's been ten days since the incident outside the school and six since the crash. No one has heard anything about Álvarez. At this point, every bit of evidence, or lack thereof, points to the two incidents being random and in no way connected." Victor didn't seem convinced.

"Do you really believe that?"

"I don't know what to believe. I only know you've been almost a prisoner stuck inside the house. Today is your birthday, and I want to do something special for you."

That faint sound I heard was another crack in the wall. If Victor kept this up, he'd shatter it into oblivion. I wasn't as opposed to it as I should be. Instead, I found myself smiling. "While it's mildly stalker-ish that you looked up my birthday, as opposed to asking me, the reason behind it is probably the sweetest thing anyone has ever done for me."

His expression turned serious. "I plan on showing you how important you are, Estelle. I don't want you to go a single day without knowing that I care about you."

A lump grew in my throat and my eyes burned with unshed tears. I swallowed the rock and sniffed back my emotions. I didn't want to ruin this moment by bawling like a baby. My mouth opened and closed several times, but I couldn't get any words out. Not that I even knew what to say. Which was a good thing, because all the ones I tried got stuck. Thankfully, Victor broke the silence. "Tonight, when I pick you up, we're going on a date to celebrate."

I was glad for the change in topic. "Where are we going?"

"It's a surprise. Just be prepared to have a good time."

I wrinkled my nose. "I've never been a big fan of those, you know."

They were never usually good ones. At least not in my experience.

"That's because you've never had me surprise you," Victor boasted with an infectious smile.

It wasn't actually true. He surprised me each and every day. None of them had been terrible yet, so maybe he had the right of it.

"Okay then. Bring on the surprise." His boyish excitement was contagious.

"Let's get you to work then so we can go out later and have some fun."

M<small>Y EXCITEMENT LEVEL</small> had grown all day until finally, I was practically dancing with anticipation by the time the school bell rang. My students had barely cleared the room before I grabbed my bag and dashed out the door.

Looking as sexy as always was Victor. I could see the power in his every move as he leaned up from his truck he'd finally gotten back. He moved with fluidity and a grace I hadn't truly appreciated until this exact moment. My fingers burned with remembrance of touching all those muscles under that black leather jacket he was wearing. The crisp early November air was cool against my heated cheeks. I expected we should start to see a lot more colder days. We'd already had one small snowfall. But it was November in Chicago. No matter how much we wished otherwise, winter, and snow, were coming.

I threw myself into Victor's arms, planting a giant kiss on his lips. I'd thrown all caution to the wind and planned on fully embracing this thing between us. I loved kissing him and had no plans on stopping any time soon now that I'd started. I was pretty sure, based on the returned exuberance, Victor had no problems with that.

"I take it you're ready," he chuckled after I'd finally let him up for air.

"Let's get this party started."

He helped me up into the truck, and soon it became clear we were heading downtown. I couldn't contain my curiosity about where exactly we were going though.

"So, you gonna tell me now where you're taking me?"

Victor glanced over at me as he pulled into the parking garage. "You'll see," he continued to tease me.

His hand was warm in mine as we walked down E. Illinois Street. Soon it became obvious where we were headed. I hadn't been to the Navy Pier in several years. In fact, the last time I'd been here was with Ines. We strolled down the path, Victor clear about his destination. He opened the door, and we stepped inside, the heated building taking off the slight chill I'd gotten on our walk over. Soon we were standing at the counter of *Frankie's Pizza by the Slice*.

"This was my favorite place to eat growing up. Even more than *Giordano's*," Victor told me.

I stared at him in complete disbelief. "That's blasphemy right there. No pizza on this earth can match *Giordano's*."

"*Frankie's* sauce is absolute perfection. The flavor. The amount on each piece. It's like magic happens inside my mouth when I take a bite."

"Magic, huh?" I chuckled.

Victor nodded matter of factly. "Complete and absolute."

"Well, it's obvious I've been eating the wrong pizza all these years then."

"Definitely. Don't worry, I'll have you converted before you know it."

I left him with the illusion that he could. After a few bites, I was forced to admit the pizza was pretty damn good. Still not *Giordano's* good, but I was willing to concede that *Frankie's* was a close second.

"Don't eat too much, we're not done yet."

"Now you tell me." I groaned.

Victor chuckled. "Come on."

We strolled, hand in hand, further along the pier. I'd always enjoyed being a people watcher and here was the perfect place for it. Families with their kids wandered around, a few of them obviously tourists by the wide-eyed expression on some of the children. The way their heads swiveled back and forth as they tried to take everything in.

There were small and large groups of young women walking together in their stilettos and dresses like they planned to head to the dance club later. Guy friends probably on their way to the sports bar to watch some football.

Then there were the couples. Young and old walking hand in hand. Enjoying time with their partner. So many people in love. I stepped closer to Victor and laid my head on his shoulder as we walked. I couldn't remember ever feeling this at peace.

We stopped midway down the Pier. I glanced at the building signage. *Amazing Chicago's Funhouse Maze.*

"What is this place?" I'd seen it before, but I'd never been inside.

"You'll see."

Laughing, I let Victor drag me inside. Holy shit, it was psychedelic. Black lights, fluorescent lights, a mirror that distorted our bodies. It was exactly what the business name described. We walked across a wooden bridge inside a tunnel of purple glowing lights. Our balance was challenged as he and I meandered across a bouncing, moving floor only made more challenging by the crazy lightshow going on. I couldn't remember having this much fun before on a birthday.

I got a little claustrophobic trying to squeeze through the "Big Squeeze". The walls were so close together you had to go through sideways. I was thankful for the hold Victor had on my hand, because otherwise I may have panicked. Out of breath from laughing, we finally reached the end of the maze. I collapsed in a fit of giggles against him.

"That was a blast. Thank you so much for bringing me here."

"You're welcome. The night's still not over."

"Damn, what else do you have planned?"

Victor winked. "Just wait."

Our next stop was no less spectacular than everywhere else. I didn't care how cold it was outside, nothing stopped me from eating ice cream. It was crazy how much Victor had remembered about me.

"After you," he gestured.

Of course, I ordered mint chocolate chip and he ordered his weird rainbow flavored concoction.

"You want to find a place to sit or you want to keep walking?" Victor asked when he handed me my cup.

"I'm okay with walking. It's getting dark, and I love looking at all the lights across the water."

"You got it."

We stood there eating our ice cream watching the riverboat paddle around the lake. It was chilly, especially right next to the water, but even with all the hustle and bustle around us, it was so peaceful out here. Chicago was my hometown. The place I'd grown up. But here, tonight, with Victor it was like I was seeing the place in a different light. Everything was brighter. Bolder. Better. All because of this man beside me.

We finished our ice cream and found a trash can to toss our garbage in. He stood behind me, wrapping his arms around me tight, and holding me close as we stared out over the water.

"Thank you so much for tonight. It's been absolutely amazing. One of my best birthdays, if not *the* best, ever."

Victor kissed the crown of my head. "You're welcome. I'm glad you've enjoyed it."

We didn't exchange any more words, merely stood there comfortably. A burst of wind crashed through us, and I shivered.

"Let's get you out of the cold." We headed back in the direction of the parking garage, but then Victor made a sharp beeline to the right. "One last thing before we leave. You're not afraid of heights, are you?"

I shook my head. "No."

"Good."

After a short wait in line, he handed our ride tickets to the employee and he helped me into the temperature-controlled, Plexiglas-windowed car. The Centennial Wheel was the most popular attraction on Navy Pier. The two-hundred-foot Ferris wheel had been around only a few years.

We reached the pinnacle, and I gasped. "Oh my god, this is spectacular."

Almost the entire city was visible, the lights glowing so brightly it almost hurt my eyes. There was Sear's Tower, its color-flashing antennas rising up from the roof like they could touch the sky. I didn't care that they changed the name to Willis Tower. To me, it would forever be called Sear's Tower. There was the John Hancock building. My head swiveled back and forth, and my eyes widened taking in the whole city lit up like a million stars in the sky. This, *this right here*, was magical.

Not caring that the entire car rocked with the force, I threw myself into Victor's arms.

He caught me with an explosion of air. "Whoa."

I hugged him as tightly as I could. He returned it with

equal fervor. I pulled back so our eyes met. "This has definitely been the absolute best birthday I've ever had. Thank you isn't enough."

The wall inside my chest was shaking, on the verge of crumbling down. When it happened, because I could already feel the foundation begin to crumble, it was going to be epic.

"I'm sure there are far more inventive ways you can show your appreciation."

A laugh burst out of me.

"Maybe *you* need to show *me*. You know, in case I get it wrong."

"It would be my pleasure."

He yanked me fully onto his lap, my legs spread as I straddled him. I rocked my hips, grinding against his erection. In return, his lips crashed against mine. An electrical charge seared me from the heat of his mouth. His tongue didn't beg entry, it took. Victor owned every inch of my mouth. Before the night was over, he'd own every inch of my body. Maybe even my heart.

Pleasure consumed me. The taste of his mouth was sweet and fruity. His hair was soft between my fingertips. But the heat of him. The heat soaked all the way through me culminating into a fiery storm that threatened to combust any second. My hard nipples ached, and I rubbed them against his chest creating a delicious friction that slammed into my core. Time stood still.

"You two might want to take that somewhere a little more private."

We broke apart, gasping for air. The Ferris wheel operator stood there with the door of our car open, an amused expression on his face, exposing us to a small crowd of onlookers peering around him. *Has anyone actually died of embarrassment before?*

Gathering what little dignity I had left, I climbed off Victor's lap, straightened my shirt and brushed my hair back with my fingers. I exited the car first, with him hot on my heels.

Spine straight, I stood proudly, grabbed his hand and smiled at the operator. "Thanks for the tip."

Victor was quiet as we walked down the sidewalk toward the parking garage. I turned my head to look at him. He returned my stare, silent, his expression worrisome. The crinkle between his eyes was adorable.

"Are you waiting for me to freak out?"

"Most definitely."

"Please," I chuckled. "I managed to survive being caught half-naked, wrapped in nothing but a sheet, coming out of your room by your dad. At least this time I was wearing all my clothes."

Victor gave a shaky laugh. "I should have known better."

"Really, though, there are worse things. You could have been balls deep inside me," I deadpanned.

He burst out laughing and tackle-hugged me, swinging me around once before setting me on my feet. My laughter joined his. We stared at each other, our chuckles slowly fading away.

"You could be, you know," I said softly.

"I could be wha—" his eyes widened in realization.

Ding! Ding! Ding!

"Are you sure?"

I nodded. "I'm sure."

This moment was eleven years in the making. At sixteen, it began as a whisper. At twenty-seven, it was a roar. Every time I looked at him, the desire grew. This was a huge step for me, because this wasn't someone who was going to leave before morning. This wasn't going to be casual. It was going to be feelings and emotions. It was going to be *Victor*. That made all the difference.

"I have a confession to make."

"What's that?"

Under the streetlight, his face seemed to flush. "I had zero expectations for tonight when I did this. Okay, so maybe a little hope, but no actual expectations. I promise." He paused.

"Okay," I prompted.

"I might have booked a lakeview room at the W Chicago."

I blinked. That was definitely not what I'd thought he was going to say. I let the news sink in for a second and examined my feelings about it. I believed him when he said he didn't have any expectations. That wasn't Victor's style. He would never have assumed I was going to jump into bed with him, no matter how our relationship was progressing.

He kept staring at me expectantly. No doubt waiting for me to get upset or angry at his presumptuousness. I wasn't though. In fact, now that I knew we had the rest of the night to ourselves, with complete privacy, the giddiness of anticipation was barreling through me. I needed to let him off the hook. With a single step, I pressed my body against him. His heart beat strong beneath my palm.

"That's an awfully fancy hotel room to be wasting money on if we aren't going to use it."

He shrugged. "I don't care if I lose the money. That isn't what this is about."

"I know," I agreed. "But if you're going to spend that

kind of cash, I have no intention of leaving that room until I have to."

I stood on tiptoe and whispered in his ear. "I hope you can keep up."

Pulling away, I walked backwards, a cheeky grin on my face. Victor stood there with a dazed expression on his face. I crooked my finger, beckoning him to me. He shook himself and barreled forward. "Oh, I can definitely keep up."

He threw his arm around my shoulder, and we walked the mile to the hotel. Each step made the anticipation grow. On our walk up to the front desk, the marble floor shone brightly under our feet. I gazed around the lobby while Victor checked us in. Everything sparkled in here. I tilted my head backwards, and the mirrored ceilings sent my reflection back to me. The place reeked of expensive decadence.

I smiled to myself. I was going to have so much fun dirtying the sheets.

"Ready?"

I pivoted at Victor's question. He held his arm out, and I looped my hand through the bend in his elbow. The elevator ride was quick. We reached our room, and Victor let me in. I flipped on the light and gasped. The room was magnificent. I hurried across the plush carpet to stare out the window. There was a perfect view of the lake and the Navy Pier. It was spectacular. I'd never appreciated how beautiful the city was at night until now.

A whisper of air dashed across my cheek as Victor swept my hair over my shoulder and kissed the spot where my shoulder met my neck. I leaned back against him with a sigh of contentment. This moment, right here, was perfection. I turned and wrapped my arms around his neck.

"I don't suppose you ordered champagne and chocolates?" I grinned up at him.

"I think I have something better in mind."

"Oh yeah?"

Victor reached over my head and pulled the curtains closed, shutting the entire world out, leaving just the two of us together in this room. He lowered his head, his lips stopping a hairsbreadth from mine. My tongued darted out to lick my lips. He was so close, it flickered against his as well. That was all it took. Our mouths crushed together.

This was what a kiss was supposed to feel like. Overwhelming. Explosive. All-consuming. It completely took my breath away. I was drowning in sensation. My lungs burned with the need for air, but I didn't want to stop kissing him. I also wanted more. Our breathing was harsh in the quiet of the room.

"You're so beautiful," Victor gasped against my lips. "I could spend a lifetime kissing you, and it would never be enough."

I wanted to tell him how I felt. Instead, I went back to kissing him, hoping he could feel the words on my lips. His palm cupped my breast, and I gasped against his mouth.

"More," I begged.

In response, he pulled my shirt up over my head before fastening his lips to mine again. Deft fingers unhooked my bra, the straps sliding down my shoulders before Victor pulled it completely off and tossed it aside. The heat of his hand burned my skin when he cupped my breast again, this time flesh against flesh. I moaned into his mouth, and he swallowed the sound.

He pulled away, and I whimpered at the loss of his touch. His chest moved rapidly up and down as he sucked in air.

My breathing wasn't any slower. The air was cold making my nipples pucker. I stood proudly before him. Victor's eyes drifted downward stopping at my breasts. His brown eyes grew darker and more heated.

He thumbed the turgid peak. My lids drifted closed at the answering throbbing deep in my belly. It wasn't enough. I wanted, no, needed more. Boldly, I took the initiative. I reached for Victor's hand and moved to the bed already turned down for us. I plucked the chocolates off the pillow and tossed them on the nightstand. I turned to face him.

"Make love to me, please," I whispered.

"You never have to ask."

His fingers made quick work of my buttons and zipper. He knelt on one knee, and my breath caught. Our eyes locked and ever so slowly, torturously, he tugged my jeans down bringing my underwear with it. Victor was so close to my wet center I could feel his breath hot against my skin. He peppered kisses along my thighs, bypassing where I needed his touch the most.

He tapped the side of my leg, and I lifted my foot off the ground. My shoe was pulled off, then the other. I stepped out of the clothes piled around my ankles. He took a tiny step back, and my eyes followed his movements. First went the shirt. I'd seen his bare chest before, but it still made my breath catch. A tiny patch of hair gathered in the middle and a thin line of hair began just below his belly button and disappeared behind the waistband of his jeans.

Things became all too real at the sight of the condom. More wetness coated my lower lips. I plucked the small square from his fingertips. I was desperate, and tired of this slow dance.

"I need you, Victor. Please."

He smiled at my begging. Strong hands gripped my waist, picked me up, and tossed me on the bed. I squeaked as I landed. Before I could catch my breath, his now-naked body covered mine. Lips melded together. Our bodies rubbed together, skin to skin, our flesh heating in the surrounding cool air. Two pairs of hands explored, learning where to touch to give the most satisfaction. Moans of pleasure and purrs of ecstasy echoed throughout the room.

Victor's thumb found my clit, and my back arched at the sharp tingle that shot through me. Adept fingers circled my wet entrance, gathering up moisture, before dipping inside. In and out, slow then fast, his fingers thrust, hitting a spot inside that made my toes curl and my legs quiver. My body tightened, and my orgasm tore through me, shards of pleasure splintering into a million pieces through me. I trembled from the release.

I heard the crinkle of foil and looked down to see him slide the rubber down the length of his cock. My mouth watered in anticipation. My legs spread and he settled into the vee. Victor's forearms caged my head, and he stared down at me with an intensity in his pitch-black eyes.

"You're mine, Estelle. And I'm yours. Forever and always."

I blinked back tears at the words that sounded so much like a vow. If I thought that kiss had changed everything, I was about to be proven wrong. A single word sealed our fate.

"Yes."

Ever so slowly, Victor entered me, tiny tremors still vibrating through my center, until he was fully seated. I wrapped my legs around him and thrust upward, trying to generate friction. Answering my call for more, he withdrew and pressed forward, rocking his hips against mine, filling me so full I gasped from the sensation. My nails scored his back, and he groaned.

Our eyes never left each other's as our pace increased, the tension building inside me again. Sweat slicked skin slid back and forth, my hair sticking to my damp forehead. Faster and faster we moved, the pressure growing. Victor reached between us and his fingers rubbed the bundle of nerves. With only a few flicks of his digit, my body tightened, and my back arched as the second orgasm ripped through me. I screamed his name. Victor continued his frantic pumping until he went rigid and exploded, the veins in his neck taut. He collapsed on top of me, his weight heavy yet comforting.

My fingers traced up and down along his back, and I buried my nose in his neck, inhaling the scent of sweat, sex, and musky male. He tried to withdraw, but I tightened my legs around him.

"Not yet. Just stay right there for another minute. Please."

Victor remained still but took some of the burden of his weight off me. Finally, I could feel his muscles straining, and I released my grip on him. He rolled to the side, but pulled me with him. He turned his head and pressed his lips to my forehead.

"I'll be right back. I promise."

Victor took care of the condom and slid back into the bed, cradling me in his arms. I needed to get up as well and use the bathroom, but I wasn't ready to move quite yet. I wanted to savor this feeling of utter wholeness being in his arms. Over the course of the last twenty minutes, the entire foundation of the wall I'd built around my heart finally crumbled and the whole thing had come tumbling down. It lay in a pile of ash and dust within the walls of my chest, and I was coming to terms with what that meant.

Victor tipped my chin up, and I met his gaze. I swallowed at the emotion I saw shining back at me. I was a coward, because I wasn't ready to hear what he had to say. He opened his mouth and closed it again. He opened it a second time. "I—I hope that was the icing on top of the birthday cake."

I let out a shaky exhale. My heart ached, because deep down, I knew that wasn't what he'd been about to say. Tears burned behind my eyes. I blinked them back and smiled instead. "It was the chocolate icing on top of a chocolate cake surrounded by scoops of mint chocolate chip ice cream."

His lips turned up in one corner. "I know how much you love mint chocolate chip ice cream."

I swallowed. "I really do love it."

Neither of us were talking about ice cream.

CHAPTER 22

I'D JUST REACHED the time clock to punch out for the night when I heard someone call my name. "Yo, Victor."

My eyes scanned the room and landed on Gladstone leaning back in his office chair. He waved me over.

I dropped into my chair on the opposite side of the desk we shared. "What you got?"

His too tight uniform pulled across his shoulders as he crossed his arms looking fully relaxed, if not smug. It was his favorite position. I kept waiting for the day his seams split apart. "I got some news on our friend, Álvarez?"

I jerked forward. "What? Why didn't you call me?"

His calm down gesture pissed me off. I'd been waiting almost two weeks for this information. This was fucking important.

"I just learned it myself. I knew you were on your way. Nothing was going to change in the ten minutes it took you to get here."

"That's not the fucking point, Jonathan. What's the news?"

"Álvarez has been found in Mexico. It looks like the Feds extradited him back here to stand trial. From the sounds of it, he hasn't set foot on American soil in the last six months. It looks like your friend's snatch and grab attempt a couple weeks ago might have been some random thing."

My mind raced with the implications. I stared my partner down. "Are you sure?"

Somehow, in the disorganized mess on his desk, Gladstone located a sheet of paper. His eyes scanned the page while he read. "Some D.E.A. agent by the name of"—he squinted—"shit, I can't make it out. Anyway, an agent who's actually working in Mexico, apparently inside the Sinaloa Cartel, said that he'd been taken into custody."

"Aren't they rivals? And why would an undercover agent be calling us?" I kept trying to make the pieces of this puzzle fit together, but nothing was making sense.

"There've been rumors that there's a traitor in their midst, and it's not the agent. Someone scorned who'd been making new deals with Álvarez. Supplying him with more drugs to sell and making him a fuck ton of money. Someone with a grudge against Salazar had apparently opened up shop down there, and Álvarez was his biggest customer. Salazar found out and reported his whereabouts to the Feds. Eliminate the competition once and for all, I guess."

Christ. I didn't know what to believe. If this were all true, then the chances of Estelle being Álvarez's target had just been shot down. It most likely was a random incident. I was relieved, of course. This meant she didn't need to stay at the house any longer. She could go back to her own place. After her birthday, things between us had changed. We'd become so much closer. More intimate. I was scared that her leaving would add distance between us. A distance we just closed.

"Earth to Victor. You listening? Your girl is safe, man. This should make you happy."

Pasting a smile on my face, I nodded. "I *am* happy. Like you said, it's great news."

I reluctantly rose, no longer quite so eager to leave. Estelle was no doubt asleep, but the morning would be here soon enough, and I'd have to tell her.

"MORNING." She strolled in and headed straight to the coffee maker.

"Morning," I mumbled.

As always, she was beautiful. Her blonde hair was pulled up in a ponytail that bounced as she walked. Her ass was the perfect peach. She moved around the kitchen, graceful and unhurried. It was a sight I'd never grow tired of seeing.

"You're staring."

I blinked and met her eye. "I'm sorry, what?"

Her hands wrapped around the coffee mug, holding it against her chest. "I said, you were staring."

"Sorry," I shook of the daydream. "We need to talk."

The mug stopped halfway to her lips before she lowered it. Her expression became guarded. I gestured to the table. "Why don't we sit."

"Actually, I'm fine right here, thank you." She was rigid, as though bracing herself for bad news.

"Sorry, that sounded ominous didn't it? I think you'll be happy with my news. Promise." I tried to make my smile encouraging, but based on her narrow-eyed gaze, I'm not sure I succeeded.

"Sit. Please."

Slowly, she followed my lead and lowered herself into the chair. She still clutched the coffee mug tightly between her palms.

"What is this alleged good news you have for me?"

"I got word last night that Álvarez has been arrested in Mexico. Where he's been for the last six months." There, I'd done it. I'd managed to get the words past the knot in my throat.

Estelle seemed to puzzle their meaning out. I saw the moment it clicked. "Does this mean that it wasn't Álvarez behind the attack on me? Am I able to go back home then?"

"It would appear that way. The evidence we have at the moment points to this being a random act. Or, if not random, you were the wrong target in the first place."

Her entire body relaxed, and she let out a huge sigh filled with relief. Then Estelle scrunched her face up. "What about the vehicle that crashed into us? Or the one that rammed into us first? What about that?"

I honestly had no idea. I couldn't connect the dots.

"I don't know. It doesn't make sense for the incidents to happen so close together, but without a suspect in either case, there's not much to tie them together."

Estelle was silent, thinking, for a minute. Then her gaze bore into mine. "Answer me honestly. Do you really think it's safe for me to go home?"

My gut said no, but no matter how much I wanted to, I couldn't prove it wasn't. I could only answer the best way I knew how. "Most likely."

"You're still not sure, are you?" It was a little scary that she could read me so well.

"Not entirely, no. But since our only potential suspect has just been eliminated, there's not much else to say."

Estelle reached across the table and laid her warm hand on top of mine. "Just because I'm leaving doesn't mean anything is going to change between us. Other than we won't have to be quiet at night anymore."

I snorted. "I don't think we're all that quiet now. I was afraid you were going to wake Pablo up last night. The way you were carrying on."

"What? Me?" Estelle shook her head in vehement denial. "You were the one grunting and groaning like you had a bad case of the trots."

"The what?" I sputtered. The image was so ludicrous, I could only burst out laughing. I waited until she set her mug down, and then I tugged her arm pulling her out of the chair and onto my lap.

"Victor," she squealed.

She clutched my shoulders on her landing. My grip tightened on her hip to hold her still, mostly because of her ass wiggling against my cock. She froze and stopped moving. I loved the flush that crept up her cheeks as she stared at me.

"You feel what you do to me? I constantly have a hard-on when you're near." I brushed back the few stray strands of hair that framed Estelle's pink-tinged face. She didn't glance away. Boldly she locked eyes with me, almost daring me to do something...more.

"If we weren't in the middle of the kitchen where my father or brother could come in any second, I might be tempted to show you how irresistible you are."

I swear I tasted blood biting back the groan that threatened to escape when she shimmied a little. Her breath was hot against my cheek as she whispered in my ear. "If we weren't in the middle of the kitchen where your father or brother could come in any second, I might let you."

"Good god, will you two give it a rest? I have to listen to you at night. Please don't make me listen to you at the breakfast table too." Pablo walked past us and opened the fridge.

Estelle scrambled off my lap and plopped onto the chair next to me, her face beet red. "Sorry."

"Hey," I grumbled. "Don't apologize to him. He's just jealous he doesn't have a beautiful woman to hold at night."

Without skipping a beat or even turning to look, my brother stretched his arm behind him, flipped me the bird, and continued scavenging in the fridge. Despite her embarrassment, Estelle chuckled beside me. It wasn't long before my dad joined us. I sat there for a minute, watching everyone. This was my family. The people I loved the most.

I looked at Estelle. She hadn't been ready for my declaration of love the other night. It shone in her eyes. The hope was there. But so was the fear. Which was why I'd altered my statement. I could wait though. The perfect moment would come, and she'd be ready to hear it. Maybe even say it back. Until then, I'd keep showing her how much I loved her, and that no matter how much it scared her, nothing would change that.

CHAPTER 23

FINALLY, I was going back to my own house. I was both excited and nervous. I wanted to be back in my own space. Especially if Victor and I were going to continue making love. I most definitely didn't want another accidental run in with Ernesto. Once had been embarrassing enough. It also made me a little nervous. I was worried that not being in such close quarters anymore, Victor and I wouldn't keep working so hard on this relationship. Or rather that *I* wouldn't. That I'd fall back into old behaviors.

That was my biggest fear. That instead of growing closer together, we'd grow further apart. Victor would be picking me up soon to take me home, so I needed to grab my things and get going. I quickly finished grading the last few spelling quizzes and then packed up. I waved goodbye to Willie on my way out the door.

Like always, Victor leaned against his truck. I took him in and my heart raced. Especially seeing that smile. I skipped across the parking lot and threw myself in his arms, slapping a big juicy kiss on his lips.

"Damn, I could get used to that type of greeting," he said once I released my hold on him.

"Well, don't. I was just feeling sorry for you standing here all alone."

He swatted my ass.

"Ouch, damn it." I rubbed the stinging spot and stuck my tongue out. Happiness poured over me. I'd forgotten what it felt like.

"You ready to go home?"

"Yes." I almost bounced in the seat.

"Manuel's going to meet us at your house. Check and make sure that no one has been inside and planted any type of surveillance equipment or listening devices while you've been staying with us."

That threw me for a loop. If the cartel wasn't responsible for the attempted kidnapping of me, then why would there be anyone spying on me? My excitement dimmed a little. Nervousness returned to take its place. "Do you think someone did?"

"It's just a precautionary measure. I know the evidence points away from Álvarez, but that doesn't mean he hasn't sent someone to spy on you. You can call me paranoid or single-minded, but I'm not taking any chances with your safety. Even if it makes me look crazy."

Put that way, it was sweet and lovely. It made my insides dance a little. "Thank you for watching out for me."

He threaded his fingers through mine. "Thank you for not fighting me on it. It really does make me feel better. I want to do everything I can to protect you."

He brought my fingers to his lips and kissed my knuckles. The spark that was always present every time Victor touched me traveled up my arm and settled deep in my core.

This was what had been missing from my life. Someone who truly cared about me. I took this feeling and wrapped myself in its warmth. Then I tucked a little piece of it inside the memory box that grew fuller by the day. The same way my heart was.

Manuel was already in my driveway by the time Victor and I pulled in. My house was a small, bright yellow bungalow style ranch. The shutters were white and matched the tiny stake fence I had lining the perimeter of my small flower garden bordering my front porch.

It wasn't fancy but it was home, and I loved it. I was curious to know what Victor thought of it. He'd never seen the inside. I had a feeling the whole place was going to feel different after he'd been in it. His scent would be in here even if it didn't linger for long. I'd probably picture him in my space long after he walked back out the front door.

Manuel greeted us as we approached his patrol car. "I did a quick scan around the perimeter to check for any weak points of entry. Everything seemed secure from the outside."

He and Victor shook hands. "Thanks."

"If you're okay with it, I'm going to grab my equipment and start going through the place," Manuel asked me.

"Of course, do whatever you need to do."

He nodded and headed back to his car while Victor and I went inside. At an initial glance everything seemed in order. I cringed a little at the dust swirling in the rays of sunshine that filtered through the mini blinds. There was also a thin layer of it on my entertainment center and coffee table. I dumped my bag on the side table.

"Things seem a little less strained between you and your brother today."

He glanced over at me from his position he'd taken near the fireplace.

"Yeah, I took your advice. Talked to him about everything."

I moved next to where he stood. The urge to be close to him grew more every day. I intertwined my fingers with his. They were strong and warm. "You don't know how happy that makes me. Do you feel better having gotten it off your chest?"

"I do actually. We haven't acknowledged it really, but he's definitely been making a concerted effort to treat me differently and thinks before he speaks to me. We're working on it."

I was glad. Manuel stepped back into the house. His eyes darted to Victor and me holding hands, but he didn't comment.

"I'm going to start in here and then make my way to each room in the house. Shouldn't take me longer than fifteen or twenty minutes."

I smiled at him. "Thanks so much for doing this. It probably won't lead to anything, but it does make me feel a little safer."

He nodded. "It's no big deal. You're probably right about not finding anything, but I know none of us, Victor especially," —he gestured in his brother's direction— "wants anything to happen to you."

I loved this family. They were the kind of family a lot of people, me included, wished they grew up with.

"Thank you, Manny. I really appreciate it."

Victor tugged my hand. "Come on, let's go in the kitchen and let him work."

He directed me to the table, sat, and pulled me onto his

lap. I didn't even hesitate or try to rise. This was exactly where I wanted to be. In Victor's arms. Instead, I settled in and laid my head on his shoulder.

"Are you glad to be home?" His breath ghosted across my cheek.

I nodded. "I've missed this place. Having my things near. Sleeping in my own bed."

"My bed already misses you."

I raised my head to meet his smiling eyes. Always the flirt. Time for some turnabout. Leaning close, I whispered in his ear. "Maybe we can use mine instead."

Victor groaned and his grip tightened on my hip. "Don't tease me like that, woman."

"Who said anything about teasing?" I wiggled my butt a little, torturing us both in the process. Especially with Manuel being only a room away. He was liable to walk in here any minute to continue his inspection of the house. I knew I was playing with fire, but I wanted to feel the burn.

"Oh, shit, sorry. Didn't mean to interrupt."

We both jumped guiltily at Manuel's apology. I rose up off Victor's lap, smoothing my pants, trying to act nonchalant. He stood as well but stayed pressed against me.

"You didn't interrupt much. Estelle was just whispering sweet nothings in my ear."

"I really was actually," I confessed.

Manuel laughed while Victor choked behind me. *That'll teach him,* I smiled to myself.

"Oh, seeing you two together is going to be even more fun now. Brother, you better watch your step around her. She is a spunky one."

Victor pulled me tighter against him. "You know she's

never let me get away with anything. I don't expect it to start now."

His brother chuckled. "You're probably right."

Manuel went to work in the kitchen using some type of intermittent beeping wand to scan surfaces, including under the table, inside the light fixtures, and around picture frames on the wall. While he did his thing, I scrounged around in the freezer trying to find something to fix for dinner. Tomorrow would be soon enough to clean out the fridge. I didn't want to throw already spoiled stuff in the trash for it to stink. Victor leaned back against the counter staying out of the way.

"I'm finished in here. I'll go check the rest of the house. You two kids behave while I'm gone." He smirked and shook his head as he disappeared out the entryway.

"Are you planning on staying for dinner?" I poked my head around the freezer door to look at Victor. There weren't a lot of options in here, and if he was staying I needed to figure something out.

"That depends."

"On?"

"Are you on the menu?" He waggled his eyebrows and I choked out a laugh.

The heat rose from my chest up through my cheeks. My fault for walking right into that one. An evil thought drifted through my brain. I closed the freezer door and stalked toward him, praying Manuel stayed busy a few more minutes. Victor tracked my every move until I pressed myself against him. My hand traveled from his chest down past his stomach. His eyes grew heated and his breathing shallow. I dipped my hand inside his jeans and stopped at the root of his cock. His nostrils flared and his eyelids drooped shut. The groan he let out rumbled through me.

"Only if you're dessert." I gave a little squeeze and removed my hand before turning around and heading back to the freezer. I happened a glance over my shoulder in time to see him adjusting the impressive bulge straining against his zipper.

"Dammit woman. Now I'm going to have to try and get rid of this damn hard-on before Manuel gets back."

I blew Victor a kiss. "Sorry."

I wasn't.

In the end, I grabbed a frozen pizza. It was too late to try and thaw anything out anyway.

"I've checked the entire house and couldn't find anything, so it looks like you're in the clear." Manuel wandered back into the kitchen. I reached up and kissed his cheek.

"Thank you for everything."

"You're welcome." He clasped Victor's hand and pulled him in for a brotherly hug. "Call me if you need anything else."

"You got it. Thanks, bro."

We followed Manuel out to the living room, and I locked the door behind him. No sooner did I turn around than Victor had me backed up against it, slamming his mouth down on mine. The kiss was possessive, reminding both of us that I was his. I loved the roughness behind it, especially when he tangled his fingers through my hair and gently tugged my head at an angle and deepened the contact.

My fingers clutched at his back and the fabric of his cotton shirt was soft to the touch. He continued his sensual assault as though imprinting his taste on my lips forever.

Victor was owning me, and I was helpless to resist it. It was all consuming. His flavor was better than any mint chocolate chip ice cream. It was intoxicating and habit-forming. No intervention in the world would cure me from the addiction to it.

He pulled back and rested his forehead against mine, both of us gasping to catch our breath. My nipples were hard enough to ache, and if Victor touched me right now, he'd find me slick with wetness.

"I didn't like you touching Manuel," he growled, his eyes boring into mine.

"It was a tiny token of my gratitude. You know it didn't mean anything. Besides, he's married." I was still breathless so it was difficult to get the words out.

"Don't care." His voice was rumbly.

"Is that why you went all caveman just now?" I didn't want to admit that I liked it. A lot. Victor's zealous reaction was hot as hell and totally turned me on. I never imagined I'd be aroused by that type of aggressiveness, but holy shit was I ever.

"No one touches you but me." His grip tightened on my hips, and I bit back a moan.

"I don't want anyone touching me, but you. I'm also a jealous girlfriend, so you better not be touching or even looking at another woman either." Even now my blood pressure was rising, and I was feeling rage-y at the thought of him with another woman. My hands curled into fists against his waist.

Victor raised his head from mine and stared down at me with a peculiar expression. "Are you?"

"Am I what?" I asked, confused.

"My girlfriend?"

I blinked and recalled what I'd just said. *Whoa.* This was about the time my defenses usually rose back up. Normally, right about now I'd be stepping back and putting distance between us. The desire to do that was missing. I was actually really happy where I was. My eyes locked on Victor's.

"Yes." My answer was confident, strong, and left no doubts.

He sent me the half smile that I used to find cocky, but now found utterly endearing. "Good, because I don't know if I can let you go."

The longer I spent with him, the more I didn't want him to let me go. And that scared the shit out of me.

CHAPTER 24

I'D TRIED CALLING Preston to let him know about Álvarez's arrest and that we didn't need to try and locate him anymore, but I hadn't been able to reach him. I needed to talk to Brody though. I didn't really know my sister's boyfriend beyond the few things Ines had told me. He'd been there when our brother was killed by Paulo Hernandez. Brody had confessed to Ernie that he was a government agent. That's how he'd discovered Ines' identity. Our brother told him. Once he found out she was a cop, he'd done everything to protect her. I trusted him with her life. Which was why I was waiting for him to pick up the phone. Ines had mentioned he was going to try and reach out to his former handler. Maybe she'd found some answers.

"Hello?"

"It's Victor."

"Everything alright? It's safe to talk?" I could hear the note of concern in his voice. Two calls in one week wasn't protocol.

"All clear."

"Okay, then. Talk to me. What's going on?"

"Have you talked to your old handler yet?"

"I have a call into her, but it's not that easy reaching someone when you're supposed to be dead. Even within the organization there are only a few people who know I'm alive. Give me a couple more days to see if she calls."

"If you talk to her, can you verify some information for me?"

"I can try. What do you got?"

"Apparently Álvarez has been caught and is on his way back to Chicago to stand trial."

"What? Are you sure?"

"No, which is what I need you to check on for me."

"Damn," he said on an exhale. "Nothing's been reported on the news. Of course, they don't always."

"I really need to see if she can confirm the intel."

"I would have thought Landon would call if he had been apprehended, but I know things changed after I resigned. Either way, when she calls, I'll see what intel she has."

The wait was killing me. There was nothing I could do about it though. I'd debated on telling him about the car accident, but I held back. There was no doubt he'd tell Ines. She'd fret and worry, and I didn't want that. Especially since it happened over a week ago and Estelle was fine. The two of them had enough on their plate to worry about without the added stress. There was one other thing I'd wanted to talk to Brody about.

"Did you hear Raúl Escobar is dead?"

"What? When?"

"Not sure when exactly, but rumor has it Álvarez did the honors."

"Jesus. It doesn't surprise me. I worked under him for

five years. Studied him. I knew everything about him there was to know. Escobar teaming up with Alejandro to betray him was not an insult he could let pass. He's killed men for less."

"If and when you talk to your contact, see if she can find out who the new player might be. With Álvarez allegedly in custody, someone else is bound to take over. There's been chatter that the Sinaloa Cartel is finally digging its tentacles into Chicago."

"I don't doubt it. They'd been trying to move into Juárez Cartel territory before shit went down. That was the whole reason Alejandro formed a coup. He didn't think his uncle was doing enough to stop them. If Escobar is dead, that means Álvarez has found someone bigger and better to supply him his drugs."

Which meant more of a nightmare for our city. More drugs. More death. Fuck.

"All right. I better go, but if you get a call from your handler, see if she'll reach out to me."

"I can't make any promises, but I'll see what I can do."

That last didn't make me happy, but there wasn't anything to do about it. The federal government had their own agenda, and if it didn't align with the local's, then we were shit out of luck.

I disconnected the call and leaned back in my chair thinking on my options. Right now, I was stuck. A position I wasn't too fond of.

CHAPTER 25

VICTOR WAS SPENDING MORE and more time over here. He'd actually slept over the last couple nights, but tonight he had to work a double so I wouldn't see him until tomorrow morning. Earlier, while I'd sat alone on my couch eating Japanese hibachi I'd ordered in, I was struck by how quiet it was in here. How lonely. He'd only been gone from the house for a few hours, and I already missed him. The way he made me laugh. All the tiny things he did like help me make dinner, clean up the kitchen.

The way Victor held me tight while we snuggled on the couch and watched a movie. How he laid on my side of the bed while I was in the bathroom so it was partly warm for me from his body heat before I climbed in beside him. Even the dumbest things like putting the toilet seat down without me having to ask him to. I'm sure that was Ines' doing, but it still meant so much.

I don't know why I continued fighting love. The emotion had dug its way into my heart, probably starting the night of what we still referred to as the "dinner disaster". I hadn't stuck around to hear everything Victor had said to my parents, but the savagery he displayed toward them before I rushed away was what I always pictured love to be. Even if I hadn't truly believe in it.

It seemed almost ironic that it was that night that I changed my mind about it existing. Not only had I started believing in it, but I was sure I'd starting falling in love. The night of my birthday love crashed into me head on.

I'd never minded, before tonight, the solitude of my house. In fact, I actually enjoyed it. The quiet nights sitting in front of my fire, drinking a glass of wine, and feeling at peace. Now that Victor had been here and now that he was gone, even for a few short hours, I'd never felt so alone before. His absence was tangible.

I wanted him here, with me. To spend our evenings together. And our mornings. And every hour in between. My body trembled with realization. I'd asked him to teach me that falling in love was possible. He'd done that and more. The bed felt big and empty. I was so screwed. I drifted off to that thought when a noise startled me. *Was that a door opening?* With a racing heart, I jolted upright. I sat there for a few seconds straining, listening for any more sounds. I dove off the bed at the sound of footsteps and grabbed the baseball bat that leaned against my nightstand. It was something Ines suggested when I'd told her I wasn't comfortable having a gun.

I'd tried going to the shooting range with her a few times, but the firearm always felt clunky in my hands. My palms refused to grip it well, and it made me nervous. So, I'd settled for the *Louisville Slugger*. I moved as quietly as possible and positioned myself behind the door. If it opened,

I'd be hidden behind it. My breath caught in my lungs I was that afraid to move.

The quiet continued. *Had it just been my imagination?* I relaxed the white-knuckled grip I maintained on the wooden bat. The air I'd been holding in escaped with an audible sound. A sound echoed by more footsteps that grew louder with each step. *Shit. Someone was in my house.* My grip tightened again and within seconds, the doorknob turned.

Slowly, the door opened with a slight creak from the hinges that needed oiled. There was a pause. I inched forward, bat raised. The light sifting through the slats of the mini blinds shone enough that I could make out the barrel of the gun and the hand encased in a black leather glove attached to it. I didn't wait another second.

With every ounce of strength, I slammed the bat down on the forearm of the intruder. A masculine scream tore through the air, and the gun fell to the ground. I moved around the half open door and swung the wooden weapon straight at the head of the masked man standing there. Both my arms shook with the reverberation of wood hitting skull. The loud thud echoed when his body collided with the door. Another wail of pain followed and he clutched his head.

I attempted to swing again, but the man dressed entirely in black gained his bearings and tore off down the hallway stumbling along the way. The front door slammed closed. I didn't waste another second. I grabbed my phone from next to my bed.

"9-1-1, what's your emergency?"

"Someone just broke into my house." My voice was shaky. I raced to the front door. With the bat still gripped in my fist and my phone between my ear and shoulder, I jerked the lock in place with my free hand.

"Are they still inside?"

"No. He ran out the front door when I hit him with a baseball bat. There's a gun on my bedroom floor that he had."

"What's your name and address?

I gave her my information and could hear click-clacking in the background like fingernails over a keyboard.

"Okay, I've got a patrol car on their way. Are you in a safe place?"

"I'm in my living room. The front door is locked now." My knees felt weak, and I thought I needed to sit, but I couldn't take my eyes off the door in front of me. *What if he tried to get back in?* So I stood there, frozen, staring at the brass knob, watching for it to move.

"Are you alone, or is anyone in the house with you?"

"I'm alone. My boyfriend is a police officer. Victor Rodriguez. I need him here. I need him to come home… please." My voice cracked on the last.

"We'll get a call into him. The patrol car should be there in a few minutes. You're doing great, Estelle. Just hang in there with me, okay?"

"Okay."

I could hear the faint sound of sirens. They grew louder with each passing second. I could see flashing blue lights out the window and still I jumped when there was a pounding on the front door.

"Police, open up."

"That's them. Go ahead and open the door."

"I'm coming," I called out.

Two officers stood on the other side.

"Miss Jenkins?" The short, stocky older one asked. He looked around Ernesto's age.

"Yes." I stepped back and let them in.

The operator on the other line spoke. "Alright, I'm going to let them take over from here."

"Yes, thank you."

My gaze landed on the two officers standing in the middle of my living room. I didn't know if the operator would really let Victor know what happened, and I needed him here.

"I need to call my boyfriend, please. He's a police officer." My hand gripped tightly to my phone.

The older one nodded. "While you're doing that, we were told there was a gun somewhere?"

"Yes, on the floor in my bedroom."

"Did you touch it?"

I shook my head. "No."

"Okay, we're going to get a forensics team here. Make your call quick, and then we need to ask you some questions."

My shaking finger punched the speed dial button for Victor.

"Hey babe, what's up?"

"Someone broke in tonight. The cops are here now." I could feel the pressure behind my eyes now that he was on the phone, but I blinked the wetness back.

"Fuck. I'm on my way."

"No, no, you're working. I'm okay." Hearing the urgency in his tone made me feel guilty. I was being silly, overreacting like this. The police were here. They'd do what they needed, and it would all be fine.

"Well, I'm not okay. Who are the officers there?"

I didn't even know. "What are your names?"

The second officer, slightly younger one with a tall, lanky

build and beady eyes, spoke up for the first time. "I'm Officer Brighton and this is Officer Pascale."

"I heard them," Victor said in my ear. "I don't recognize their names, but tell them I'm with the forty-third precinct under Captain Petty. I'll be there as soon as I can."

I'd calmed down and there was no longer this urgency to needing him here. I was glad he was coming, but he didn't need to rush. "I'm sorry for taking you away from your work."

"Baby, you and your safety is far more important to me. I'll go crazy the rest of the night if I don't come home anyway. I need to see for myself that you're all right."

Victor was telling the truth. He needed that reassurance. I don't know why I thought otherwise. It did make me feel less guilty.

"I'll see you soon then." All my muscles ached from the tension I'd been holding onto. With Victor on his way, I could breathe easier. I set the phone on the couch.

"Thank you for letting me call him. He's on his way. Oh, he wanted me to mention Captain Petty and the forty-third precinct. That's where he works. His name is Victor Rodriguez."

They nodded and Officer Brighton spoke up. "The forensics team is on their way to process the crime scene. I need you to tell us what happened."

My legs were still a little shaky so I took a seat on the edge of the couch. "I was almost asleep when I heard a noise. Then I heard footsteps. I jumped out of bed, grabbed my bat, and when the intruder stepped through my bedroom door, I whacked him a few times. He escaped out the front door. I called 9-1-1, and you two showed up."

"Could you tell what he looked like?"

"No. He was wearing gloves and a ski mask."

"And you're sure it was a man?" Pascale asked.

"I can only assume so. He was tall and the grunts of pain he let out when I bashed him across his head definitely sounded masculine."

"Do you know why someone would want to break into your house? Any enemies? Ex-boyfriends maybe?"

I hesitated to mention Mr. Álvarez. At least until Victor got here. The man had been powerful and all reaching. He'd definitely had police on his payroll. It didn't mean that either of these two were, or had been, but a voice told me to be cautious.

"No enemies that I know of. I also parted amicably with all my ex-boyfriends so I don't think any of them would have had reason to break in."

Brighton scribbled all the information down in his notepad.

"Where's the weapon you used?"

I pointed to where I'd leaned it against the wall.

"We'll need to take that as evidence. Check for fibers of any kind."

"That's fine."

The front door opened, and a uniformed Victor stood there with a crazed look in his eyes. They landed on me, assessing, making sure I was unharmed. The frantic expression on his face slowly disappeared. Officers Brighton and Pascale moved forward as though to stop him from rushing to me.

"You must be the boyfriend."

He merely pushed past them. I was already on my feet. Victor palmed my cheek, the maniacal fear still hovering just below the surface. "You okay?"

I nodded. "I'm fine, now that you're here."

He turned back to the officers. "Victor Rodriguez."

"Forensics should be here any minute. They'll do what they need to do and we'll be on our way. You'll be available for any more questions if we have them?" Pascale directed the last to me.

"Yes, I'm not going anywhere."

The crime scene team showed and processed the entire house. Fingerprints were taken from various surfaces. Both the gun and my bat were taken as evidence. There were no signs of forced entry. No windows broken. They concluded the intruder used a common device called a bump key to disengage the deadbolt on the front door. By the time Victor and I were alone in the house, I was dead on my feet. It was oh-dark-thirty, and I'd been up half the night. He tugged my hand.

"Come on, let's get you to bed." With a gentle touch, he helped me under the covers and smoothed my hair back.

"You going back to work?" I asked, drowsily.

"No. I was going to be off in a few hours anyway. I already notified my captain."

I said a silent prayer of thanks. As much as I didn't want him to get in trouble for missing work, I was thankful he wasn't leaving me.

"I'm really"—yawn—"glad." My eyes were so heavy.

"Get some rest." There was a feather light stroke of his lips across my forehead. "I'm going to go lock up. I'll be right back in here when I'm finished."

I murmured okay, feeling safe knowing he wasn't going anywhere, and then I was out.

CHAPTER 26

I WOKE ALONE. The room was brightly lit, with the afternoon sun coming through the blinds. After a visit to the bathroom, I went out to look for Estelle. I found her sitting on the couch reading a book with the television on, but silent, in the background. She looked tired with dark circles under her eyes and heavy lids. She'd woken up a couple times throughout the early morning hours. I'd held her close until she fell asleep again.

Hearing the fear in her voice last night was something I never wanted to experience again. I don't know how dad did it after mom died. If anything happened to Estelle, I don't know if I could survive without her. It didn't matter if she didn't love me back yet. It wouldn't change my feelings for her. I'd love her until I drew my last breath.

I took another step forward, and the floor creaked. Her gaze darted up to meet mine. She smiled and set her book on her lap. "Hey. You sleep okay?"

"I did, thanks."

"Did your captain give you a hard time for rushing over

here last night and not finishing your shift? I'm sorry if I caused you any problems."

I sat on the couch next to her and pulled her close. "You didn't cause any problems at all. He understood. Dad and I both work under him, and he knows what family means to us. If one of us needs the other, we drop everything. It's been like that since I joined the force."

"Family, huh?"

My lips brushed hers. "Most definitely. You're part of my family now. Which means you come first in everything."

"Well, I'm glad you didn't get into trouble."

"Even if I had, it would have been worth it."

I sat holding her close for a minute, grateful she was safe. I pulled back to look at her.

"I know the lock doesn't seem to be broken, but I want to change it anyway. Just in case. I'm going to run out and get a new one. Do you want to come with?"

Estelle hesitated. "No, I'll be okay."

"Are you sure?"

"I'm positive. I live here. I'm not going to let some unknown person scare me so much that I can't stay by myself for an hour. I'll be fine. I've got my book to keep me occupied."

"I won't be long. I'm also gonna call Manny and see if he can stop by in the next couple days and install a security system. It will make me feel better." I didn't expect Estelle to protest, and I was glad she didn't.

"Thank you. I'll feel better too."

"I'll be back soon."

I quickly ran to the hardware store and picked up a new deadbolt and chain lock for a little bit of extra security. Within an hour I was back at Estelle's.

"Everything still all right?"

"I'm good. A little hungry, but otherwise okay."

I held up the bag in my hand. "Give me a little bit to install these and then maybe we can order in and watch a movie."

"Sounds good."

Estelle went back to her book while I worked on replacing the lock. I caught her watching me occasionally. Once I installed everything, including the chain lock, I checked everything out to make sure it all worked.

"That should do it." I held out my palm where both keys laid. She hesitated for a second and only picked up one. Her bold stare met mine.

"Why don't you keep the other one."

My gaze bounced back and forth between her and the key in my hand. "Are you sure? This is a huge step."

She nodded gravely. "I know. I'm a little freaked out about it. But it also feels right. I don't do relationships, yet here I am. I'm going full force forward with this whole thing. If this is too fast and too weird for you, you can tell me. I'll take the spare key too. And now I'm regretting this, because you probably feel obligated to take it since I just kind of thrust it—"

I smothered the rest of Estelle's words with my mouth. Her awkward babbling had been adorable, but there was no way I was letting her think that I didn't want that key. I'd been holding back a little, taking my cues from her. She just bulldozed her way forward, and I had to keep up. I didn't mind in the least. I took a final sip from her lips before pulling back.

"Does that answer your question on whether I want it or not?"

She blinked appearing a little dazed. Finally, her eyes focused and locked on mine. Then she smiled. "I guess it does."

"Good, now, why don't you go relax. I'm gonna grab something to drink and then we can order food."

I grabbed a glass of water and sat next to her on the couch. Maybe other men my age were hanging out at bars or clubs and having the time of their life. This right here though, sitting with my woman close, getting ready to eat together and watch a movie was what I called perfection. I'd never been a club kind of guy anyway. I wanted quiet nights at home. Even not so quiet ones if it involved the sounds of kids laughing and being happy. That was the kind of life I wanted. And I wanted it with Estelle.

"Where do you want to order from?" I asked her

"I don't care. Why don't you decide?"

"Anything in particular that you're in the mood for?"

"I'm not sure. Wherever you pick I'm sure I can find something on the menu."

"Okay, what about barbecue?"

She wrinkled her nose. "No, that doesn't really sound very good."

I glared at her. "Seriously?"

Estelle's lips twitched before she burst out laughing. "I've always wanted to do that. You should have seen your face."

"Woman," I growled right before I tackled her. I pinned her down on the couch, her entire body shaking with laughter. "What am I going to do with you?"

Her expression grew serious. "Love me?"

"I do love you." The words just came out. I hadn't planned on saying them, but now that I had, I wasn't taking them back. "I love you more than I ever thought possible. It's okay if you need more time. I'm not going anywhere."

A sheen covered Estelle's eyes, but she quickly blinked it away. She swallowed once. Then twice. I didn't have to hear the words from her. I knew. Instead, I leaned down and kissed her, tasting them on her lips. Our tongues tangled. She responded with passion, clutching at me, pulling me tighter to her. Her moves were desperate and frenetic. She yanked at my belt, making quick work of unbuckling it. She tugged at my jeans, pulling them down.

"Please," Estelle begged, thrusting her pelvis upward. "Please."

I shifted onto my knees on the floor and worked her pants down, the need for her catching fire. I wanted to take it slow, but she wasn't having it. She pulled me back to her, spreading her legs, the left one falling off the couch. I half collapsed on top, settling against her heated center. She braced her foot against the floor and thrust upward again.

I hissed at the contact. In a single move, I positioned myself and plunged into her wet pussy. Estelle screamed as I pistoned in and out, her nails digging into my ass, urging me to go faster. Her teeth nipped at me, and I crashed my lips down on hers, lost in the frantic passion that slammed into me.

The sound of skin slapping against skin rang in my ears along with Estelle's cries for more. My orgasm rose inside me. I needed her to reach hers first. My hand found its way between us, and I rubbed her clit, hard and fast, generating the friction needed to send her over the edge.

Her moans and pants grew louder. Her body trembled and then with another two flicks of my thumb against her, she screamed as the orgasm rushed through her. She jerked beneath me, her teeth biting her bottom lip. The sight pushed me over the edge, and with one hard forward lunge, my cock exploded, bathing her insides with my seed.

Estelle's pussy clenched down, milking more and more of it from me. I shuddered against her neck, my tongue flicking against her skin to lap up the salt from her sweat-dampened skin. My lips brushed her ear, and I whispered those three words into her ear. "I love you."

ESTELLE WAS fast asleep in bed. I was out in the kitchen cleaning up. Just as I finished washing the last cup, my phone rang. I didn't recognize the number, so I let it go to voicemail. A minute later, it rang again. With a groan, I answered.

"Hello?"

"Is this Victor Rodriguez?"

"Can I help you?"

"My name is Landon Roberts."

Landon. Landon. Where did I know that...Shit, this was Brody's former handler at the D.E.A.

"I understand you've been looking for Miguel Álvarez," she broke the silence.

"Yes. I assume Brody has filled you in on everything?"

"He did. He said that there was an attempt made to take a family friend a few weeks ago."

"That's correct. Also, I don't know if it's related in anyway, but a few days after that a vehicle rammed into us. Then last night someone broke into my girlfriend's house."

"I assume this girlfriend is the family friend in reference

to the other incidents." There seemed to be a tone of exasperation in her tone.

"One and the same."

"Jesus," she cursed under her breath. "First Brody and now this."

I refrained from commenting, because it sounded like she was talking to herself. There wasn't anything to say anyway. She focused back on me and our conversation.

"It's quite possible all three are connected. Word has traveled through my organization that Álvarez has put out a call to bring the woman to him."

"I thought he'd been captured in Mexico."

Landon was silent. Then she broke it. "Mr. Álvarez has, in no way, been taken into custody. He is currently still at large. And not in Mexico, either."

"Wait a minute. Are you telling me he's here? In the city?"

"If you were told he'd been apprehended, then it would seem as though you've been given incorrect intel."

I paced the length of the kitchen. "Three days ago, I was told explicitly that he was on his way back to Chicago to stand trial."

Landon huffed out a breath. "I'm not sure who told you that, but Miguel Álvarez is most definitely in Chicago, somewhere, and has been for the last three months, based on an extremely reliable source we have inside."

Jesus Christ.

"Mr. Rodriguez?"

I shook myself. "Call me Victor."

"All right then, Victor. Who told you about this alleged arrest?"

"My partner."

"I see. Well, I can't speak to that. But he is most definitely Stateside."

Fuck. "Do you have any idea where exactly he is?"

"If we did, we would have arrested him. I have someone attempting to gain information on the inside, but after what happened with Brody, Álvarez is being extra cautious."

"So what does that mean?"

"It means that until we get more intel, my hands are tied."

Which didn't help us in anyway. "Thanks, I appreciate it."

"I wish I had more news."

"This was at least something more than I already had."

"You have my number. I can't guarantee I'll be able to do anything, but I will try my best to assist anyway I can."

"Thanks again."

"Good luck."

I set down my phone. I needed to talk to Jonathan, but it was too late to call. I'd sort it all out tomorrow before our shift started. Needing to be near Estelle, I turned out the light and headed to the bedroom. I quickly disrobed and crawled under the covers. She murmured in her sleep, and I pulled her tight against my chest. Her body relaxed against me. I laid there for at least another hour thinking about what I was going to say to my partner tomorrow. The little bit of sleep I managed to get caught up with me and my eyes grew heavy. The sound of Estelle's steady breathing soon lulled me into a restless slumber where I tossed and turned half the night.

CHAPTER 27

HAD it really only been yesterday that Victor told me he loved me? A day since I hadn't said it back? The words had clogged in my throat. I was so pissed at myself. It was like I kept waiting for everything to fall apart. Not that I was an eternal pessimist or a glass half empty kind of gal, but the cynic inside me kept whispering in my ear. Taunting me.

Her voice grew louder with each passing day, chipping away at this happiness inside me. She whispered things like how it was only a matter of time before Victor disappointed me. Before he changed his mind. How he didn't really love me. In the end, we'd only grow to hate each other. *Man, my inner cynic was a real bitch.*

I ignored her and went out to the front room to find Victor. He was sitting, stone-faced, on the couch.

"Morning." I leaned down to give him a kiss.

"Hey."

I stopped at his tone. "Is everything okay?"

Was he regretting telling me he loved me? I could feel a

burning in my eyes. Had I fucked things up between us? He pulled me onto his lap, but I couldn't relax.

"I got a call last night from Brody's former handler, Landon."

I blinked. "What did she want?"

"According to her, Álvarez was never arrested, and he's in Chicago somewhere."

"Oh my god. So it *could have* been him behind everything after all?"

"Yes. She said he's allegedly been here for three months."

"What are we going to do?"

"I'm going to take you back over to our house, and then I'm going to figure out what the hell's going on."

Knowing that Álvarez had been so close all this time had me terrified. It had to have been one of his men that had broken in two nights ago. I climbed off his lap.

"Let me go pack some things."

"Okay. I'm going to call my dad and let him know."

I hustled into the bedroom and threw clothes and my toiletries in my bag. I'd just unpacked and here I was packing again. Would this nightmare ever end? Once I was satisfied I had everything, I went back out into the living room to hear the tail end of Victor's conversation.

"Yes, sir. I'm on my way." He slammed his finger down onto the phone screen. "Fuck."

"What's wrong?"

"That was my Captain. There's a lead on Álvarez's whereabouts. Someone spotted him in the north side of the city. My boss is sending us over there right now. He's going to have a patrol officer stop by and keep an eye on you until I can get back. I'm also going to have Manuel come by as well. Will you be okay until the officer gets here? Shouldn't be long."

"I'll be okay. The door will be locked, and I'll engage the chain."

"I don't want to fucking leave, but he said to get there ASAP."

"Don't worry." I laid my hand on his arm. "It'll be fine."

"Okay. I love you." He kissed me, and then bolted out the door.

For the next twenty minutes I alternated between pacing, something I seemed to have picked up from Victor, and sitting on the edge of my couch. I hadn't been lying when I said I was okay. I really was, but it was still slightly nerve-wracking knowing Victor could be going into danger.

My doorbell rang. That had to be the patrol officer he said was on his way. I peeked through the curtain to see who it was. I recognized the light-brown haired man dressed casually in jeans with a black t-shirt and black leather jacket over it. It took me a minute, but I got the chain unlatched and the door unlocked.

"Looks like you drew the short straw." I opened the door and stepped back. "Come on in."

Officer Gladstone didn't say anything for a minute. He just casually strolled around my living room stopping once to pick up a picture frame, glance at it, and set it back down.

"Can I get you something to drink? I have orange juice or water. That's about it."

He looked up, and I shivered at the darkness in his eyes. Something wasn't right.

"No, thanks."

He stepped closer to me, and my brain screamed danger. I backed up, slowly.

Then he spoke again. "You are the key, you know."

I spun and dove for the door. The knob turned, and I tried to jerk it open. Only a sliver of sunlight peeked through before it slammed right back shut with the force of my body being thrown against it. Gladstone's vicious fingers snatched my hair and yanked my head back. The tendons and muscles of my neck screamed in pain, and I hissed in agony. He pressed himself against me, pinning me against the wood with no room to move or defend myself.

"You really did a number on Martín the other night. Broke the poor bastard's arm."

"Good," I spat out. "Too bad I couldn't bash his brains in."

He chuckled evilly. "Bloodthirsty bitch aren't you? It's kind of hot."

Gladstone rubbed his erection against me. I tried jerking away. He yanked my hair harder, and tears burned my eyes. "Mr. Álvarez is anxious to speak with you."

"I told you before, I don't know anything."

His lips touched my ear, and I shuddered in disgust. "You may not, but Victor does. Which means you're coming with me. Oh, and in case you get any ideas…"

The gun rammed into my side spoke volumes. "Keep your elbows to yourself. Álvarez wants you alive. Didn't say anything about slightly damaged."

Gladstone loosened his grip on my hair, and my head throbbed. His hand skimmed down my side, pausing for a moment at my breast, before traversing down. He wrapped his hand around my hip, his fingers far too close to my center, and ground his cock against my ass again. I swallowed back vomit.

"I see why Victor likes you."

"Go fuck yourself." I refused to let him see my terror.

Before I could blink, he'd snatched my hair again and slammed my face into the door. I cried out in pain and felt warm wetness drip from my nose.

"You have a smart mouth for someone in your predicament. That right there was just a love tap. Talk to me like that again, and I'll cut out your fucking tongue. You got me?"

I swallowed back my tears and nodded. With fingers still clutching my hair, Gladstone jerked me away from the wall.

"Let's go. Don't forget, I *will* shoot you if you try anything."

He dragged me out of the house and into his car. The gun he kept jammed against my side was incentive for me to do what he said. The only thing keeping me sane right now was Victor. I needed to stay alive long enough for him to find me. And he would. I had to believe that. I couldn't die without telling him how I felt.

"Why are you doing this?" I asked from the passenger seat.

My eyes remained on the scenery in front of us as we left my neighborhood.

"Working for Mr. Álvarez is a lucrative business."

I glanced over at him and the gun sitting in his lap. He caught my eye. "I wouldn't try it if I were you. I'd hate for this thing to go off accidentally."

My eyes darted away. *Why were we heading out of the city? Where was he taking me?* I needed to keep him talking.

"So you're betraying your partner and the entire police force for money? How original."

The sarcasm was lost on him. "Money talks. What can I say?"

"How long have you been a dirty cop?"

"Tsk, tsk," Gladstone scolded. "Such name calling. I think of it more as a business venture really. Easy work for really great pay. I don't plan on slumming it inside a raggedy old patrol car for the rest of my life. Waiting for some lowlife to gun me down because I'm wearing a uniform. I'm saving for early retirement."

"You're a piece of work." He disgusted me.

Gladstone only laughed. "Be that as it may, but I'm a rich one."

The car slowed and turned down a narrow alley. Burnt out and rundown warehouses surrounded us on both sides, blocking out any sunlight that may have tried to reach the ground. It was dark and ugly down here. We stopped in front of a blue metal building. He honked the horn in a series of long and short beeps. Within seconds, the garage door slid up. We crept slowly forward into the darkened abyss. The second the back fender breached the threshold, the door slid back down, locking us inside.

Dim fluorescent lights barely illuminated the interior of the building, some flickering and creating an almost strobe light effect. It was like the static on your TV. Standing on the concrete floor in the middle of a room were several men. It was the one in the center that commanded my attention. I'd seen pictures of him on the news before, but none of them did Miguel Álvarez justice.

Gladstone parked the car and gestured with the gun. "Time to get out, sweetheart."

My fingers trembled against the door handle. I stepped

out and stood next to the car, not daring to move closer to the threat in front of me. It didn't make a difference, because he came to me.

Upon closer inspection, he was just as handsome. I had to tilt my head back to meet his eyes. I could barely pick out the flecks of gray in his dark hair. His face was almost free of any age lines, so it was difficult to tell how old he was. Under any other circumstance, I'd appreciate how attractive Álvarez was. Instead, I shook in fear, because this man was deadly.

"Martín tells me you're a *un demonio*. How do you say… she-devil, *si?*"

Was I supposed to answer the question or was it rhetorical? I chose to remain silent.

"I understand you do not know exactly where that traitorous *puta* is, but you are her best friend. This means you are important to her." He traced a path down my cheek with his finger. I flinched at the touch and jerked away. Álvarez grabbed my face in his hand, squeezing it so hard I was afraid he was going to break my jaw. I whimpered in pain as the tears poured. "You may not know where she is, but she knows where you are. She will come to your aid, and when she does, I will kill her."

He shoved me away from him. I stumbled backward and fell on my ass. Rough hands jerked me back to standing, fingers digging painfully into my arms, dragging me through the warehouse. It was stupid to resist. There were worse things they could do than kill me. The two men who handled me threw me into a metal chair in the middle of a small room off the warehouse floor.

I gagged when a piece of fabric was shoved in my mouth.

My hair got caught in the knot he made to bind the gag making me wince. Rope wrapped around my body. My wrists were bound behind me, my ankles bound to the legs of the chair. There was nowhere for me to go. I didn't want them to see my fear. I tried desperately to hold back the tears, but I could feel them slide down my cheeks anyway.

CHAPTER 28

"Son of a bitch."

The fucking lead had been a dead end. My phone beside me rang. *Manuel.*

"Hey, are you at Estelle's yet?"

"Victor, you need to get over here. Now," he barked out.

I jolted upright in my chair. "What's wrong?"

"She's missing. There aren't any signs of a struggle, but there's a small smear of blood on the back of the front door."

"Fuck. I'm on my way."

I disconnected and raced through my call history. My thumb slammed down on the entry I was looking for. While the phone rang, I dodged in and out of vehicles, gunning the engine and speeding past them, cursing to get out of my way, with a desperate need to get to the house. There was no doubt in my mind that Álvarez had her.

"Yes?" My sister answered.

"He has Estelle."

"Oh my god. Are you sure?"

"Last night, I got word from Landon Roberts that

Álvarez is in fact back in Chicago. Has been for months. Someone also broke into Estelle's house late the other night."

"Damn it, Victor, why didn't you call me?"

"Because I didn't want you to worry. Manuel is at her house. I'd had to go on some bogus call following an alleged lead on Álvarez's location. A patrol officer was supposed to go over there and stay with her until I got back. I'd also asked Manuel to go over there. He's the one who discovered her missing."

"Where are you now?"

"I'm on my way to her house. Let me call you back when I find something out."

"You better. You have to find her, Victor."

"I will. Gotta go."

I skidded to a screeching halt in Estelle's driveway. Manuel opened the door before I even got to it.

"The door was unlocked when I got here. No signs of forced entry."

Just then my cell phone chirped signaling an incoming text. I didn't recognize the number, but there was a video attachment.

Estelle was gagged and tied to a chair inside a room. The blank white brick walls behind her did nothing to help to discern her location. The video zoomed in on her face. Tears streaked her cheeks and her nose looked bloodied. I roared out my anger. Thirty seconds had barely gone by before my phone rang. Same number from the text.

"If you harm a fucking hair on her head, you're dead."

"I don't think you're one to be making any demands, *señor*," the caller spoke with a heavy Spanish accent.

"What do you want?"

"Ines Rodriguez. As you can see from the video, I have a

guest. I propose a trade. You give me what I want, and I give you back what you want."

"Ines isn't here. I don't know exactly where she is," I hedged.

"Then my guest is of no use to me. *Adíos*."

"Wait! Wait!"

"You have remembered something, I take it?"

Fuck his condescending tone.

"It's going to take a few days for her to get here. She's not close."

"You have twenty-four hours. I will call again with instructions soon."

"Hello?"

He'd hung up. I roared and moved to throw the phone across the room, but Manuel stopped me.

"Don't let him get to you like that. We need to be smart about this. Now, what did he say?"

I tried to focus on slowing down my breathing by taking in a few cleansing breaths. Finally, I got my rage under control. "We have twenty-four hours to get Ines here. No mention of Brody. I'm not sure if that's intentional or if Álvarez still thinks he's dead."

"Let's go in assuming he knows Brody's alive."

"God damn it. I need to call Brody's handler."

Manuel nodded. "Do that. I'm calling *papá* and Pablo."

I found Landon's number again.

"Agent Roberts."

"It's Victor Rodriguez. Someone's taken Estelle. I got a video sent to me by text. She's alive. They called shortly after I received it. We have twenty-four hours to set up an exchange. Estelle for Ines."

"Son of a bitch. Did he mention Brody?"

"No."

"Do you have a number where the text and call came from?"

"I do. It's not a local number though."

"Send it to me. Forward me the video as well. Let me see what I can do. I'll call you later."

I disconnected the call and sent her everything. I paced the floor, pulling at my hair in frustration.

Manuel had already disconnected his call. "Dad and Pablo want us to meet at the house. There's nothing we can do until we hear back from Álvarez."

"Don't you think I know that?" I snapped, then quickly regretted it. "I'm sorry."

He clapped me on the shoulder. "Don't be. I can't imagine how you feel right now. But, Vicky, we're going to find her."

I swallowed hard. We had to. "Let me lock up here and we'll head to the house."

For several minutes, I stared at the house key in my hand. Had it really only been yesterday since Estelle had given this to me? A single day since I told her I loved her? Jesus, it seemed like a lifetime ago. With a shaking hand, I inserted the key and locked the door. Manuel and I jumped in our vehicles and headed to our father's house.

INES AND BRODY were on their way back to Chicago. It had been a quick phone call, especially once they heard the demands. It would take them about fifteen or sixteen hours to get here from Colorado, which left us only a small window of time to formulate a plan. I'd spoken to my captain and let him know everything that was going on. From Jonathan's incorrect intel on Álvarez to Estelle's kidnapping. He was prepared to organize a special task force, including a S.W.A.T. team. I let him know we'd be in touch once we got more information. I prayed there was enough time for backup. We still didn't know where she was or where the exchange was supposed to take place.

I hadn't sat down since I got that video. A lot could happen to Estelle in a single day. I'd been testy and short-tempered all night. It wasn't long before everyone left me alone. My phone rang a little after eight p.m.

"Hello?"

"Bad news. There's nothing in this video or in the call that indicates this is Álvarez. Not once was his name mentioned. I didn't expect it to be." Landon sighed, and I knew that wasn't the end of it. "I talked to my superiors. Without proof that it's Álvarez, the D.E.A. isn't going to risk their time and resources on a kidnapping that doesn't directly tie into the cartel. Especially one that doesn't involve drugs or an exchange of products. What they're calling a simple kidnapping of some random woman is going to be left to the locals."

Fucking federal government. This meant we were on our own. "And there won't be time to get some type of back up if we do confirm it's Álvarez."

"Which I'm sure is his intent."

Something had been driving me crazy about this whole thing from the beginning. "What purpose does it serve him to take Estelle? Also, what about that rumor regarding Raúl Escobar? Can you confirm Álvarez was behind it?"

She hesitated. "I really shouldn't share—"

"Landon," I interrupted.

"Let me finish."

I sighed in frustration.

"I shouldn't be telling you this, but Álvarez *was* involved. It would seem that there was a minor uprising within the Sinaloa Cartel."

"What kind of uprising?"

"I don't know all the details, but from what our agent on the inside is reporting is that a woman by the name of María Luisa Velasquez has taken Escobar's place."

Well, that was one hell of a surprise. "Since when does a woman become one of the biggest drug suppliers in Mexico? And why the fuck would Álvarez form a partnership with her?"

"Since she was the one who killed Escobar. Apparently, our friend María Luisa is the much younger half-sister of Emilio Salazar, who runs the Sinaloa Cartel here in the States. Salazar sold her when she was fourteen to one of his associates. She was not treated well. Three months ago, she murdered her husband and turned on the cartel."

Christ. "So, she betrays her half-brother's organization by joining forces with Álvarez. She then kills Escobar to prove her loyalty and to take his place."

"That's essentially the gist of it. Our inside agent says that Señora Velasquez made a lot of powerful connections while under her husband's roof. He was not a well-liked man with plenty of enemies."

"That still doesn't explain why Álvarez would take Estelle."

Landon's laugh was humorless. "Loyalty is the cardinal rule within the cartel. You break that rule, you're dead. Brody and Ines broke that rule. Law enforcement or not, to Álvarez, they were a part of his syndicate. Part of his family. They betrayed him, which means they have to pay."

She paused for a moment before delivering the final blow. "Álvarez has no plans to stay in Chicago permanently. He won't risk imprisonment. His chances of staying hidden and running his business from Mexico are much higher than if he returned. Like you said, he'd be arrested, mostly likely convicted based on the evidence, and sent to a maximum security prison like Pablo Escobar. He won't take that chance. Álvarez is here for one thing, and one thing only. To kill Ines, Brody, and anyone else that stands in his way of retribution."

"Son of a bitch."

"Look. On the record, there's nothing I can do."

"And off?"

"I was barely out of Quantico when I was assigned to be Brody's handler. I didn't understand a fucking thing about what being deep undercover meant. Yet this guy, one who didn't know jack shit about me, entrusted his entire life to me. He may not work for this organization anymore, but there's not a chance in hell that I'm going to let him down now. Whatever help you might need from me, I'll do whatever I can."

I hadn't expected that. "Thank you. We'll call you when Brody and Ines get to town. We're supposed to get a phone call with instructions before the trade."

"You best start getting ready now, then. You're going to need some major firepower. There's no telling how many men Álvarez has with him."

"We'll handle that."

"You got it. I'll be around, just call me when they get here."

"Will do."

Finding Estelle may not be a priority for the D.E.A., but it was priority to me. We'd find her with or without them. I had no idea how, but failure was not an option. Álvarez wanted Ines. He must not have learned his lesson when Alejandro tried to get rid of Brody. You hurt someone we love, you weren't just up against one person, you were up against all of us.

CHAPTER 29

MY LEGS HAD FALLEN asleep ages ago. The pain of pins and needles each time I tried to move was excruciating. My arms and hands didn't feel any better. Gooseflesh dotted my skin, and I couldn't stop the chills that raced through me. I didn't think there was any heat in this place. If there was, it certainly wasn't in this tiny room. I hadn't thought it could get worse than that, but I really had to pee too.

Álvarez had been absent since I'd been brought here, but I also hadn't heard the warehouse door open. It was possible he was still out in the building somewhere. Or the room they were holding me in might just have drowned out the sound of it. The not knowing was driving me crazy. Then again maybe being unaware was a good thing.

Shortly after I'd been tied to this chair, Gladstone had come into the room with a tripod and an old handheld video camera. He hadn't spoken a word to me while he set it up. Once he'd finished, he turned, his gaze running up and down my body causing a different type of cold chill. Especially when he paused at my chest. I'd swallowed back the bile threatening to rise. He didn't touch me, but he sent me a cocky grin. One I wanted to slap off his face. Or see Victor do it. Then, he left and hadn't been back since. I'd sat here, alone, cold, and terrified. Manuel had been coming over to stay with me until his brother got back from his call. *How long after I'd been taken had Manny shown up?*

A rattle sounded across the room. My eyes jerked to the doorknob before it opened and Gladstone stepped through. He was alone, which made me nervous. I swallowed hard.

"How you doing? Hanging in there, I see. It's showtime, so I hope you're ready for your cameo."

He moved across the room and adjusted the angle of the video camera. His face disappeared behind it for a second before resurfacing. "This little home movie is for Victor's viewing pleasure. After he receives this, he's going to get a short phone call. I hope your friend and her boyfriend hop in their car or on the first plane and get here soon. If not, you're not going to be quite so pretty for my old friend Vicky."

I stared at the camera, waiting for something to happen. A little red light blinked, signaling it was recording. I held my breath. *Was there going to be some type of performance?* Gladstone wasn't wearing a mask. There was no way he would want his face shown in connection with this video. It was the only thing that gave me any consolation. So long as no one else joined the show.

My focus centered on that blinking red light, waiting for it to go dark. I started counting— one Mississippi, two Mississippi, three. I tried not to shift or fidget in any way. Especially if this video was going to Victor. More than ever I wanted to appear strong for him. To show him that, at the moment, I was okay. *Sixty-Mississippi.* The red light went off.

Gladstone rose, pulled out the memory card, stuck it in his pocket, and left the camera where it was. The sick feeling in my gut returned with a vengeance the closer he got to me. He traced a path down my cheek with his finger, and I jerked away. If the gag hadn't been in my mouth, I'd have tried to bite the digit off. I didn't see the back of his hand coming, he moved so fast. My head snapped to the side and a stinging pain spread across my face.

He grabbed my hair and jerked my head back. *Goddamn it, enough with the hair pulling.* I roared out my pain and rage behind the gag. The sound turned to a choked cry when Gladstone roughly squeezed my breast. Tears poured down my face. His breath smelled like stale coffee.

"This can go really easy or really hard for you. It all depends on how nice you are to me."

He eased off both punishing holds he had on me. Instead of painfully squeezing, his touch gentled and he began kneading my breast in almost a caress. I whimpered at his touch. Gladstone's hand drifted lower and lower. My breathing sped up, and I squeezed my eyes shut. A buzzing noise screeched across my eardrums. Then he was no longer touching me. Fuzzy voices filtered through until finally I could hear them clearly.

A man stood in the open doorway, yelling at Victor's partner in Spanish. Gladstone barked something back, shot me a heated glare, and stormed past the other man. After sending me a look of disgust the second man closed the door behind him. Left alone, I broke down sobbing.

Once I was all cried out, I steeled my spine. No way was I letting that piece of shit break me. No matter what he did to me. The only thing I had to do was survive until Victor got here.

CHAPTER 30

THE SOUND of raised voices drew me out of sleep. I'd fallen into bed sometime around two or three this morning. Only because I knew that if I was going to be of any use to Estelle, I needed at least a little bit of rest. I rolled out of bed, threw on the pair of jeans I'd tossed over the back of my gaming chair, and headed downstairs. A glance at the clock said Brody and Ines should be here any minute. Unless the sound I heard meant they were already here.

I followed the voices, one of them definitely Ines', toward the den. The entire family was present, including my sister and her boyfriend. My father and Ines paced, while Brody, Manuel, and Pablo were seated. Ines had never looked so frazzled. Not even while she'd been undercover looking for Ernie. It was obvious from the bags and dark circles under her eyes, she hadn't slept much either.

"Hey," I greeted them.

Ines spun and ran into my arms. "I'm so sorry, Vicky. This is all my fault."

I squeezed her hard, before pulling back. "No, it's not.

None of us could have guessed how this was all going to go down."

"So, does anyone have a plan?" Pablo spoke up.

"Álvarez has specifically asked for me. I'm going in first."

Brody rose from his seat. "No, you're not. We already talked about this."

My gaze darted between the two of them who were facing off against each other.

"No, *you* talked about this. I should be the one. Then he'll have two women who he most likely will underestimate."

"Exactly," he raised his voice in exasperation. "Álvarez knows that we'll do anything to protect you both if he has you under his control. That makes you a liability."

Hurt dashed across Ines face. Brody was right though.

"Besides," he continued. "You can't think that any of your family is going to let you go first after they find out you're pregnant."

"You're what?"

Ines' hurt glare bore into her partner. I'm sure that wasn't the way she'd wanted us to find out. She turned her gaze to meet all of ours. "I'm only about three months. Just because I'm going to have a baby doesn't mean I'm not capable of taking care of myself."

Jesus, she was a stubborn woman. But a baby? I was going to be an uncle.

My father made his way over to Ines. Despite why we were all here, there was so much joy on his face. He cupped Ines' cheeks. "I'm so happy for you, *conejita. Yo, un abuelo?*"

Ines grinned. She'd always been our father's little bunny. "*Si, papá.* You'll be the best *abuelo* ever."

"Which means we need to keep you and *el bebé* safe."

It killed Ines to admit our father was right.

I stepped forward. "That's settled then. We still need a plan."

My grandfather had served in the Vietnam War as a military strategist. He'd taught my father how to play chess when he was a kid. Strategy was something my father excelled at. It made him the most equipped to come up with a game plan.

"We have no idea where he even is yet. We also don't know many men are with him. He's not going to call until the last minute. Which means we need to come up with several options. Brody," my father turned to the man in question. "You know Álvarez the best. What can you tell us?"

"He's smart. He'll be someplace where, if anything does go wrong, he can get away quickly. There will be a car waiting for him nearby. It's also even more likely that he'll have a boat waiting. No one would expect that escape route. Which means wherever he's stationed himself, he's probably going to be close to the lake or a river."

My father continued. "Okay, so let's assume that he's holding Estelle in one of the many warehouse districts along the lake. From the time he calls, we're going to have a tiny window of opportunity to get there before the exchange is supposed to occur. Which means we need to start preparing now. Manny, we're going to need eyes and ears."

My brother nodded. "I've got some S.W.A.T. equipment in the trunk of my car."

"Good." My father paced along the carpeted floor again, brainstorming out loud. "Manuel can work on getting that set up. Brody is going to need to be mic'd. No doubt Álvarez will find it, but the more intel we can get before that happens, the better off we're going to be."

I piped up. "Based on what Manny and I saw in the video, Estelle is being held in a room somewhere, possibly in one of the warehouses. I don't know if there are any windows in there or not. The picture was too grainy to get a clear indication of the lighting. Plus, it was getting close to twilight, so it's possible that the rest of the buildings were blocking any light coming through anyway."

"If she is in there, she's probably going to have at least one guard on her," Brody added.

"What happens once he's inside?" Pablo asked.

We all turned to our father. "We have to assume that Álvarez is going to double cross us and has no intention of letting either of them go. Brody, do everything you can to get Estelle as close to you as possible. Once she's within reach, grab her, and run. We'll cover you."

Fuck, there were so many things that could go wrong. What if there wasn't anywhere for the two of them to hide? What if Estelle was hit by a stray bullet? No, I had to trust Brody to protect her.

I glanced at the clock. We had less than five hours before our deadline. Which meant we had at least three or four before Álvarez would call.

"I talked to Landon. She's offered to help us however she can. I don't know how far the offer extends, but it was inferred that if we needed an extra hand, she'd be here. I just have to call her."

"Okay. Give her a call. Have her meet us here. We'll fill her in on our plan and then we just have to wait for Álvarez to call."

I was going crazy with waiting already. Ines reached for my hand. "We'll get her Vicky."

"I know." There was no other option.

LESS THAN AN HOUR LATER, Landon had arrived at the house. She and Brody had shaken hands and he'd introduced her to us all. Since then, Brody and Ines had been cuddling on the couch, whispering to each other. I knew they both had to be worried with him being in front of Álvarez again. They knew how ruthless he was.

Dad and Pablo had been religiously going over everything and planning for any contingencies. Manuel sat in one of the chairs, eating. Said that was when he did his best thinking. Landon had taken a position in the corner of the room. She looked thoughtful, but also slightly guarded. I'd checked in periodically with my Captain, letting him know we still didn't have a rendezvous point for the exchange. He'd said he'd try to keep the men prepped and ready to go at a moment's notice, but we were shorthanded as it was. He'd also tried locating Jonathan, but he was M.I.A. For now, his hands were tied. I'd hung up and since then, I'd done nothing but pace. The minutes felt like hours as time slowly ticked by.

The ringing phone jarred us all to attention. A quick glance at the clock said it was almost thirty minutes before the exchange. Fuck, it was cutting it close.

"Hello?"

"*Hola, Señor Rodriguez,*" the caller greeted me like we were friends.

"Where is she?"

"So impatient. Has your sister arrived?"

"Yes. Now, where is Estelle?"

"You will go to the Steelworkers Park along the lake on the south side of the city near South Works. I will call you in twenty-five minutes and give you an exact location. I wouldn't be late if I were you."

"That's not enough time."

There was no response.

"Fuck. Come on."

The six of us raced to the garage. Earlier, we'd packed two cars full of weapons, ammunition, AV equipment, and bulletproof vests. Brody, Ines, and Landon all rode with me while my brothers rode with our father. Chicago traffic on a good day was a mother fucker. With blue lights flashing, we sped down the interstate, weaving in and out of cars, blaring our sirens to get them to move.

With barely enough time to spare, we made it to the park. Within moments of our arrival, my phone rang. I put it on speakerphone.

"Across the north slip are six warehouses. *Señorita Rodriguez* will go to the third one. Upon her arrival, she will knock on the east side entrance. She will come alone. If anyone arrives with her, I will kill everyone. Once the exchange is made, the other *señorita* will walk out the same door. She will have one minute to get out of range or she will be dead. You have ten minutes."

Before the call even ended, we all took off running. Breathless, we darted through the warehouse parking lot, weapons drawn, ducking behind dumpsters and stacks of pallets, staying low, trying to remain hidden. We all skidded to a halt against the west wall of the second warehouse.

"Here, put this in your ear," Manuel shoved a small earpiece at Brody, who complied. Then he clipped a tiny gadget to the button on his shirt. "This is a camera. I'll be able to hear and see everything you do."

"Brody? Victor?"

We all spun, weapons aimed in the direction of the whispered voice. *What the fuck?*

"What in the hell are you doing here?" Brody barked.

Preston stepped out from behind a nearby dumpster. His eyes scanned all of us, pausing for a minute on Landon. He drew back, eyes wide in surprise, but quickly shook it off. He returned his attention back to his brother.

"This is where Álvarez has been hiding out. I've been staking out the place, waiting to see if he comes back. Once he did, I was going to call you."

"Jesus," I shook my head. "He's already in there. With Estelle."

"Fuck, are you serious?"

"Yes. You need to get out of here before you get us all killed."

"I'm not leaving."

"Look," I barked. "We don't have time for this. Preston, I don't care what you do as long as you stay out of the fucking way. Understand?"

Preston nodded, gravely. "I understand. I swear on my mother's grave I won't do anything to endanger Estelle's or my brother's life."

"Fine. Now is everyone ready?"

We watched Brody take off at a lope before disappearing around the other side of the building. Manuel pulled up his monitor so we could see what was happening through the camera attached to him. We knew there was a chance shit could go south the second Álvarez laid eyes on him. We'd run out of options though.

Brody knocked on the door. It opened to a man pointing a gun straight at him. He was jerked inside, and that's when we got our first look at what we were up against.

CHAPTER 31

NEVER IN MY life had I been so exhausted. My eyes were gritty like sandpaper. I'd forced myself to stay awake for fear that Gladstone would come back while I was sleeping. Not that it would have made a difference if he had. But it made me feel better thinking it would. The same man who'd stopped him from his assault yesterday had entered a couple of times and let me use the bathroom. For a blip of a moment, I'd thought about trying to get free, but there was no way of knowing who, or what, was beyond this room. So, I'd complacently let him lead me to the bathroom and then back to this chair. I'd stumbled and almost fallen walking due to the numbness in my legs. Even unbuttoning my pants had been a challenge, but I certainly wasn't going to ask for help.

There was a tiny window near the ceiling in the room I was being held. I'd watched the sunlight fade, and I'd watched it grow bright. The only thing I could see through it was the roof of another building. While I sat here, alone, I had pictured the stars in the sky. How bright they could shine. That was the one sad thing about living in the city. You could never see how beautiful the night sky truly was. All the twinkling lights up above you. When I got out of here, I was going to ask Victor to take me on a vacation somewhere. Maybe up to Fox Lake. There were cabins we could rent. I'd have him find one with a front porch swing where we could sit with nature and see the stars reflected off the water.

We'd talk about our future. The kids we were going to have. I wanted a big family. I laughed to myself. The delirium from lack of sleep must be kicking in. Victor hadn't even mentioned marriage, and here I was, thinking about our kids. My eyes burned, but I forced back the tears. I couldn't give up hope. I trusted Victor with my life. I was absolutely, whole-heartedly in love with him. His name was a song my heart beat out.

The doorknob rattled, and I jerked. Expecting my recent frequent visitor, I was surprised to see Álvarez himself stroll in. No one would ever guess by looking at him that he was the ruthless leader of the cartel. His blue pinstriped suit was perfectly pressed, red tie smooth against his chest before disappearing behind the buttoned suit coat. Black leather shoes shone without a single spot or speck of dirt. Not a hair on his head was out of place. He strode forward confidently and with purpose. The only thing that made a person pause was his eyes. They held a savage quality.

He stopped before me, pulled down my gag, and then squatted, putting himself almost eye level with me. "I hope you've been enjoying your stay, *señorita*."

My eyes burned with hatred, but my smile was saccharine sweet. The stubborn side of me, the one that got me into trouble, couldn't resist responding. "Sadly, your accommodations leave a lot to be desired. And your turndown service sucks."

For a moment, we just stared at each other, and then Álvarez threw back his head in laughter. He wagged his finger at me. "You have a lot of fire for someone in your predicament. I could almost admire you."

Before I could even blink, my head jerked to the right and a burst of pain shot through my cheek. *Stupid, Estelle.*

Álvarez tugged his shirt sleeves down and straightened his jacket. "You're lucky I'm a lenient man, *señorita.*" He glared evilly down at me. "If you speak to me with such disrespect again, I will make your death more painful than it needs to be. *Señor* Gladstone has taken a liking to you. Perhaps I will let him teach you some manners before he kills you."

The blood drained from my face, and I cursed my smart mouth. Álvarez pivoted from me and began to move about the room with an easy stride.

"Do you know that because of Officer Rodriguez, I have no family left? No one to carry on my legacy. She killed the only blood I had left."

Even though Alejandro had betrayed him and tried to overthrow him, he'd still been Álvarez's nephew.

"Brody would never let Ines come alone. You have to know that."

Álvarez froze mid-stride, and my breath caught in my lungs. He turned toward me.

"What did you say about Agent Thomas?" His voice was low and dangerous sounding.

Why can't you keep your fucking mouth shut, Estelle?

There was no taking back what I'd already spilled. "I said that Brody will show up as well."

With three steps he was in front of me. I craned my neck back to look up at him.

"Are you telling me that Brody Thomas is still alive?"

I stared back wide-eyed. "You didn't know?"

He spun on his feet and marched out the door leaving it open.

In my field of vision was the cement floor and bright fluorescent lights hanging from the ceiling. Wooden crates piled at least eight feet high were scattered around the area. On the far side of the building was a metal wall with four-paned, dirt and grimed-covered windows evenly spaced across the width of it. They were so high off the ground it didn't matter that you could barely see through them.

Raised voices came from out in the main warehouse floor. I couldn't actually make out what they were saying, but the tone was definitely not a happy one. After a few moments, the arguing ceased. Long moments passed. I couldn't hear anything. No voices. No movement. I kept my eyes on the door waiting for someone to walk through. Shadows moved and were then still.

I didn't know what good it would do if I actually got free, but I tested my bonds, twisting and moving, trying to wiggle at least one wrist free.

"There has been a slight change of plan. It's time to go."

Álvarez stood in the open doorway. He pulled a penknife from his pants pocket and sliced my bonds. He yanked me out of the chair and then wrapped his arm around my waist. I winced at the pain shooting through all my extremities.

Before I could blink, he pulled a gun and pressed it to the side of my head. "Move."

He held me securely against him, and we walked forward and out into the warehouse. He kept pushing us further across the room. I gasped at the sight of Brody standing there. *Where was Ines?*

He smiled reassuringly at me. "Everything's going to be fine, Estelle."

His gaze shifted back to Álvarez. "Let her go, Miguel. You have what you wanted."

My captor spat at the floor. "What I want is to see you and that *puta* of yours dead."

Brody shrugged. "I already told you, you're going to have to settle for just me. Now, let her go."

Álvarez shrugged. "*Si,* that was the agreement wasn't it? She is all yours."

He gave me a small shove, and I stumbled forward. This seemed too easy. He'd already promised Ines and I were dead. Fuck. I kept moving in Brody's direction, bracing myself for a bullet in the back. My gaze remained locked on the man in front of me. He continued to smile encouragingly. I was a little over an arm's length away before everything went to hell.

"Now!" Brody grabbed my arm and yanked me so hard I felt like it was being pulled out of the socket. There was an explosion, and gunfire erupted all around us.

CHAPTER 32

"T̲H̲A̲T̲ M̲O̲T̲H̲E̲R̲F̲U̲C̲K̲I̲N̲G̲ T̲R̲A̲I̲T̲O̲R̲.̲"

"Holy shit. Isn't that Gladstone?" Pablo asked from my right.

Landon spoke up for the first time since we'd left the house earlier. "Who's Gladstone?"

"My partner."

"Wait, are you telling me your partner is a dirty cop?"

I glanced over at her. "Unless you can come up with another explanation, it appears so. He had to have been the one who took Estelle."

"Listen," Manuel hushed us.

"Tomás, my old friend. Or should I say Agent Thomas. You appear well for a dead man," Álvarez greeted Brody.

"Where's Estelle?"

"Where is your *puta*?" he countered.

"You don't have to worry about her. You have me instead."

Álvarez slashed his arm through the air. "That is not what we agreed upon."

"That is what you're going to get. Now, go get Estelle," Brody barked.

Our eyes remained focused on the entire scene. My jaw ached from the tension I was holding in it. Finally, the older man nodded. "Very well."

Álvarez turned his back on Brody, marched across the floor, and disappeared inside the open door on the opposite wall. Within a minute he reappeared, only this time, not alone. Holding her in front of him like a shield, and with a gun pointed at her head, was Estelle.

"Shit."

I took off running, knowing everyone would be hot on my tail. Muffled curses came from behind me. I skidded to a halt outside the entrance. Manuel appeared right next to me.

"Wait until Brody gets her out of the way, bro."

I watched on his screen as Estelle moved slowly forward. There was so much fear in her eyes. Inch by inch she got closer. *Three, two, one.*

"Now!"

I fired several rounds at the doorknob, and then kicked in the door. After that, chaos reigned. Like ants, we swarmed inside the building, gunfire erupting all around us. We all dove for cover, hiding behind anything that offered protection. Shot after shot was fired. Bodies fell. I spotted Jonathan diving behind a stack of wooden crates. My eyes scanned the room. *Where was Álvarez?*

"Gladstone's at one o'clock," I warned my brother.

"Got it."

A lone gunshot echoed before all was quiet. I called out into the silence. "It's over, Álvarez. There's nowhere to run. Gladstone, I know you're in here too. Both of you come out with your hands up."

"Álvarez is dead," Jonathan called out from his hiding spot. "Don't shoot."

He slowly came out from behind the crates, hands in the air, gun pointed at the ceiling, finger off the trigger. Keeping my weapon trained on him, I moved forward, alert for any movement.

"Put the gun down," I ordered.

Slowly, he bent down, arms still stretched out in front of him, and placed the gun on the floor.

"Kick it over here."

He pushed it across the floor with his foot. It slid across the concrete to land at my feet.

"A fucking dirty cop. What a waste. Why'd you do it?"

He shrugged. "I like expensive things."

I sneered in disgust. "You won't need them in prison."

Jonathan laughed self-deprecatingly. "I'll never see the inside of prison. You know that. I'll be dead before I ever make it there."

"That's not my problem."

Before I could guess his intent, he reached behind his back and pulled out another weapon. I fired round after round into him. Jonathan's body jerked, and he stumbled backwards a few steps before collapsing against the exit door. Dark red spots appeared on his chest. He slid down the door leaving a smeared path of blood behind him. His butt hit the ground and his head lolled to the side, eyes slowly drifting shut, chest not moving. I kicked the gun away from him and checked for a pulse. *Nothing*.

"Victor!"

Shots rang out. I spun on my heel in time to see Álvarez fall to his knees. Brody stood behind him with a gun in his hand. The older man stared at me in shock before toppling face first onto the cement floor. Jesus. Was it finally over? My eyes darted around the room.

"Where's Estelle?"

"I'm here." She stepped out from her hiding place.

My eyes locked on hers. She raced toward me, tears streaming down her face. I sprinted across the room, meeting her halfway. The second I reached her, I crushed her in my arms, her cries loud in my ear.

"I've got you, baby. You're safe, now. It's over." I repeated the words again and again.

Her tears lessened and the tight-fisted hold she had on me loosened. I pulled back to look at her, to reassure myself that she wasn't hurt. That she was okay. Her tear-stained cheeks tore my heart to shreds. I swiped away the wetness with my thumbs. I assessed the rest of her. Her nose was crusted with blood, and a bruise was forming along the side of her face. Otherwise, she appeared whole. She laid her palms on top of mine. "I knew you'd come for me."

Estelle's confidence in me was humbling. "I'm sorry I didn't get here sooner."

"It doesn't matter. You came." She inhaled a shaky breath. "I love you so much. I was so afraid I'd never get the chance to tell you."

"I love you too. And you'll never have to be afraid again."

The night of her birthday, even without the words, Estelle had told me she loved me. I'd just been waiting for her to admit it out loud.

"Victor?"

I glanced over to see Manny standing there.

"Sorry to interrupt, but a couple agents from the D.E.A.

just arrived. I guess Landon called them. They want to talk to all of us."

They decided to show up now? When everything was over? I shook my head in disgust.

I wrapped my arm around Estelle's shoulder and led her outside. We hadn't taken two steps before Ines screamed for her best friend. The two women embraced, both of them crying. Leaving them to their reunion, I stepped over to Landon, and two suit-clad, sunglasses wearing men with D.E.A. badges hanging from their neck, who stood a few feet away.

"Álvarez is dead, I hear," the first suit said by way of introduction.

Fuck these guys. If they'd been that concerned about taking him in alive, maybe they should have showed up before now. I shrugged. "It would seem so."

Landon's lips twitched.

Suit number one sneered. "I see."

"You're welcome to his body. He's right in there. Along with a dirty cop and four of his men." I gestured over my shoulder.

"We'll get to them. We're going to need to ask you some questions. Why don't you come to headquarters tomorrow morning, say eight a.m.? Here's my card."

I took the rectangle paper and tucked it in my vest. "Sure thing."

Without another word, the two of them walked away and into the warehouse. I turned to Landon. "Charming fellows."

"Yeah, neither Agents Brickman nor Crawford has much of a personality. Regardless of the fact that they're dicks, they're both good at their job."

233

I withheld my doubts, mostly because I couldn't care less.

"So, what happens next?" I asked her.

"The M.E. will show up and take care of the bodies. Word will spread that Álvarez was killed in a D.E.A. shoot out, and we'll all go along with it. Beyond that, who knows?"

I shook my head. We did all the work and the Feds would get the credit for it. Sounds about right. "What about you?"

Landon shrugged. "I'll go back to my desk job."

"I really appreciate your help."

"I told you, Brody did me a huge favor all those years ago. I merely paid back what I owed." She gestured over my shoulder. "You got someone over there waiting for you. Good luck to you two. You guys deserve to be happy." With that, she strode away and back into the warehouse.

I looked over to where I'd left my sister and Estelle. The whole family stood there, but I only had eyes for one person. Needing to hold her tight to remind myself she was safe, I headed in their direction. I reached her and she wrapped her arms around me. We held each other tight, and I swore now that I had her, I'd never let her go.

CHAPTER 33

1 week later

"How soon before Victor moves in?"

My head snapped in Ines' direction, and I practically choked. "What?"

She snorted and took a bite of her ice cream. "You heard me. Brody and I have been staying at dad's house this whole week, and I have yet to see my brother."

After Victor had rescued me, he'd made me go to the hospital to get checked out. Once I'd been discharged, I called my boss and requested a month-long leave of absence. I hadn't been in the right frame of mind to go to work. Plus, I didn't want to explain to my kids the bruises on my face. I was worried they would scare them.

"He was at your house yesterday."

"Yeah, while I was at the grocery store. And from what I

was told, he only stopped by for fifteen minutes so he could grab more clothes. Then he was gone again."

"It's not something we've talked about."

Ines stared me down. "Estelle Marie Jenkins I've known you for over twenty years. You, my dearest, closest friend, are full of shit," she scolded, wagging her spoon at me.

It was true though. We hadn't talked about it. There wasn't anything to talk about. Neither of us wanted to be away from the other. "Do you think it's too soon?" Ines had me worried that maybe we *were* moving too fast.

"Hey," she scooted closer to me. "I was only teasing. Look at Brody and me. We were shacking up barely three months after we met. You and Victor have known each other your whole lives. If it feels right to you guys, then it's right."

The things was, it did feel right. Like things were just falling into place. It was a little scary actually how effortless it was. I had no doubt we would still argue, strong personalities and all that, but at the end of the day, we were finally together. And in love.

"It definitely feels right."

"That's all that matters. I'm so happy for you two. Neither of you could see that you were in love with the other, but the way you both looked at each other over the years… I was just waiting for you guys to realize it." Ines laid her hand on my arm "Now you're really going to be my sister. I couldn't ask for a better one."

Damn it, she was going to make me cry. I threw my arms around her. "Me either."

The sound of the lock disengaging made us turn toward the door. Victor stepped in, pausing for only a second at the sight of Ines.

"Hey, sis," he greeted her. He walked over to us and leaned down to kiss me hello. "Hi, beautiful."

I beamed up at him. "Hey yourself."

"And," Ines drew the word out. "On that note, I'm outta here. I don't need to see my brother and my best friend making cow eyes at each other, no matter how glad I am you two are finally together."

I sputtered. "Cow eyes? What the hell is that?"

She stared at me intently and then fluttered her eyelids spastically. "It's like this flirting thing. You know, cow eyes?"

Victor chuckled, and I shook my head. "You're such a weirdo."

Ines threw her hands up in the air and stood. "I don't know what I'm going to do with you. I've clearly taught you nothing over the years. Anyway, you all go do whatever it is that you do. I'm heading home to go make cow eyes at my own man."

I rose from the couch and wrapped her in a giant hug. "Thank you for being my best friend. I love you."

"Love you too, Bubbles."

I walked her to the door and turned to Victor. Before a week ago, I don't think I fully appreciated how damn good he looked in his uniform. He was sexy as hell. And all mine.

"How was work?"

"Not bad. It was actually a pretty slow day." While he told me about it, I followed him into the bedroom. He took off his gun belt and laid it across the top of the dresser. I leaned against the doorframe and watched as he disrobed. He did it methodically, still talking to me about the drug arrests he made and the school career day he dropped by for, his fingers moving from one button to the next. It shouldn't have been a turn on, but it was. His muscles in his forearm flexed and relaxed with each move he made. Until he stopped moving.

I glanced up to find him staring at me.

"Enjoying the show?" He asked, raising his left eyebrow.

"Most definitely. I'd offer to help, but I like watching you."

Before I could blink, Victor snatched my arm and pulled me against him. He nuzzled my neck, and I tilted my head, giggling, to give him better access.

"I feel so objectified," he murmured against my skin, his lips skimming across the top of my shoulder. I pressed myself against him, moaning my approval. He moved back across my shoulder, up my neck, down my jaw, nibbling along the way until finally his mouth met mine.

Victor kissed me like he hadn't seen me for days. Like he'd counted every second before he could run home and touch his lips to mine. I kissed him back the same way. Like I wanted to memorize his taste and keep it close to me while he was away from me. It was the same every day he came home. He'd greet me with a kiss. I'd watch him get undressed, and he'd kiss me again until I was breathless.

"I missed you," he said after one last kiss. "Did you and Ines have a good time today?"

"We did. She took me shopping."

"Oh yeah? Did you find anything good?"

"Uh huh," I nodded, biting my lip and waggling my brows.

Victor perked up at this. "What did you get?"

"Oh, you know, nothing special. Just some lingerie."

His eyes heated and his nostrils flared as though scenting me. "Lingerie, you say?"

I drew patterns on his chest with my fingertip. "Yep. I thought maybe later tonight I could model it for you."

By now he was practically panting. "Hell yeah, you should."

"If you're really nice, I might even let you take it off me."

Victor gripped my hips and pulled me tighter against him. "I'll be better than nice."

I smiled up at him. "I bet you will."

He groaned. "God, what you do to me woman."

"No less than you do to me. I love you, you know." The words got easier to say every time.

"I love you too." He dropped a kiss on my forehead. "Let me change, and then we can grab something to eat. After-wards, you can give me that little show you promised."

"You got it." I leaned up and brushed my mouth across his one last time. I turned to head back out to the living room. Victor smacked my butt making me laugh. I grabbed a few things out of the fridge while he finished changing. At first I thought it would be weird having him in my house all the time, but it wasn't at all. He fit in here like he'd always belonged. His heat surrounded me before I felt his arms wrap around my waist. I leaned back against him.

"What are we having?"

"I thought I'd make meatloaf and fry up some potatoes."

"Mmm, sounds delicious. What can I do to help?"

That right there was just one of the millions of things I loved about this man. Victor did something every day to make me fall in love with him all over again. Blinking back my happy tears, because he probably wouldn't understand, I faced him.

"If you don't mind, you can peel the potatoes."

He saluted me. "You got it. Give me that peeler."

I reached into the drawer and handed it to him. We worked together with ease, chatting about mundane things. It struck me then, that I wanted this forever. It hadn't hit me until now. I stopped squishing the crackers and eggs into the hamburger.

"Do you want to move in? I mean, like for real. Not just spending the night and going back and forth from here to your dad's to get your stuff. But actually living here. With me."

Victor paused his peeling and stared at me. "Is that what you want? Because I'm okay with what we have right now."

"Yes, it's really what I want. I love you. I want to spend all the seconds of my day with you. We're practically there already. Why don't we just make it official?"

He grabbed me around the waist. He spun us in a circle. I couldn't stop laughing. We came to a stop and he kissed me hard and deep.

"I love you, too. Now, let's hurry up and get this dinner going so you can try on all the lingerie you were teasing me about earlier."

My entire life, I'd believed that love was nothing but pain and anger. I glanced over at the man at my side. At the man who'd taught me that that was a lie. Love wasn't painful or angry at all. Love was…Victor.

EPILOGUE

1 month later

LANDON. So that was her real name. Unlike the fake one she'd given me two years ago. Even after all this time, the pain I'd witnessed that night continued to lurk deep inside her eyes. I could see it from across the room. Maybe because I was looking for it.

I bet she smelled the same. A combination of vanilla and lavender. There had been moments over the last twenty-four months that I swore I could still smell it. Especially while I was high. The scent had been the strongest then. Almost like it was reminding me that that night with her had been better than any rush heroin had ever given me.

Brody had invited me over to his and Ines' new house for a housewarming party. After Álvarez's death, he and Ines had returned to Colorado and sold their small, fledgling ranch along with the few heads of cattle they owned. My brother was going to have to go back in a couple weeks to finalize the sale, but everything had been set in motion. The two of them had come back to Chicago. It was home.

I took a sip of my warm Coke, my eyes never leaving the blonde across the room talking to Brody, Ines, and Ernesto. Landon wasn't your classic beauty. Her features were too disjointed for that. It was her eyes that drew a person in. Only if they were paying attention though. I'd been watching her from the moment she walked through the door nearly an hour ago. Her gaze had met mine and her steps stuttered, but she recovered quickly.

For the last fifteen minutes Landon's eyes kept darting toward the nearest exit. She was itching to get out of here.

Finally, she snatched the opportunity. She disengaged herself from the group, grabbed her coat, and bolted for the door. Quickly, I set down my plastic cup and followed. She'd almost made it to her car before I caught up.

"Leaving so soon?" I called out.

Landon's entire body froze for a beat and then thawed. She tried to jerk the door open, but I slapped my palm across the top of it, stopping the movement. Her lavender vanilla scent washed over me.

"Move your hand." She practically growled the order, her wickedly sharp cheekbones red with anger.

She still hadn't met my eyes. I kept my arm right where it was, waiting for her to finally look at me. I counted the seconds of our stand off until finally, she raised her head and glared back. Jesus. The pain lurking behind the anger almost caused me to stumble backward from the force of it.

"Why'd you run?"

Landon closed her eyes for a heartbeat before opening them again. A shutter now covered the blue irises. She didn't prevaricate or act like she didn't know exactly what I was talking about.

"I didn't *run*. I simply left. We had a good time, and then it was over."

I crossed my arms. "Liar."

She flinched, her eyes darting away from mine. Her too thin lips flattened even further.

"You and I both know it was more than just a 'good time', Landon."

She pushed back her shoulders and stood tall on legs that went on for days. Her gaze bore into mine. "We fucked. That was it. Nothing more, nothing less."

"Does Brody know?"

Her horrified expression answered that question. "God, no. I didn't even know he was your brother until a month ago."

That's what I thought. Brody would have killed me. It didn't change the fact that there was more to what happened between us than just a fuck. There'd been a connection. "I've never forgotten you."

She swallowed, another flash of pain flickering in her eyes. "It was two years ago. You should probably get over it. I know I have."

With that parting shot, she yanked the door hard, knocking me out of the way, and dove behind the wheel. I backed away from the car, letting her escape. For now. I stood there until her car disappeared, and then I turned to head back inside.

Brody spotted me closing the front door. "Hey, where'd you go?"

"It was getting a little stuffy in here. I just stepped out on the porch for some fresh air for a minute."

His look said I was crazy. It was the end of November. In Chicago. The air wasn't fresh so much as take your breath away. An arctic front had blown through the city and brought with it unseasonably cold temps. It was supposed to warm up in a couple days, but for the moment it was bone chilling.

"Ines wants to open the housewarming gifts. You gonna stick around for a bit?"

"Yeah, for a little while."

I'd never understood the whole concept of giving gifts after people moved into a house. More than likely they already had whatever shit you bought them. How many potholders did a person need anyway?

While Ines opened her gifts, oohing and awing over them all like they were the best presents she'd ever received, my mind drifted back to that single night two years ago.

There'd been a desperation behind Landon's kisses. My fingers itched with remembrance of her soft skin. Of cupping breasts on the small side, but still beautiful. Then, there were her tears. I'd been horrified, afraid I'd hurt her. Instead, she'd achingly whispered—practically begged me really—to make the pain go away, if only for one night.

She'd fit in my arms like she belonged there. We'd made love for hours. It hadn't been some casual fuck between two strangers no matter what she said. We were two tortured souls seeking comfort from each other. Perhaps even love. I'd felt something that night. It had been visceral and raw emotion.

Despite her dismissal, she'd felt it too. I'd been right when I said she'd run. It didn't matter, because I'd found her. This time I wasn't going to let her get away.

Thank you so much for reading STRIKING DISTANCE! I hope you enjoyed it. If so, I'd greatly appreciate a review on the platform of your choice. Reviews are so important!

Turn the page for a preview of **ATONEMENT**, Preston and Landon's story.
Coming May 2020

Want to see how Brody and Ines got together?
Be sure to check out IN TOO DEEP!
Get your copy here: https://amzn.to/2O8pETl

ATONEMENT

Two years ago

LONELINESS GNAWED AT ME. Any friends I had were long gone. Driven away by my self-destruction. Clean-and-sober me tried making new ones, but going to the club, getting drunk, and finding some chick to take home and bang wasn't my thing. Which was why I was sitting in a hotel bar, on a Saturday night, drinking water.

Alone.

I was here, because otherwise, I'd be out *there*. On the streets.

The urge grew stronger every day. I could curb it for a little while, but then it would crash through me again like a tidal wave until I thought I'd drown in want and need. The water was mid-chest level, the pressure mounting. Soon, I'd be suffocating, gasping for air that was there but couldn't fill my lungs. The sensation would overwhelm me, and I'd do what I always did to get rid of it.

Use.

Anything to make me fly high above the ocean of guilt and pain. The self-hatred would, of course, follow once I landed. Then the cycle would begin again.

It had been this way for a decade. Ten long years of leaving destruction in my wake.

Four years was the longest I'd managed to fight. It seemed like eons ago.

I'd talked to my brother today, though we weren't close. Not anymore. Every time we saw each other, he'd say something which would only fuel the never-ending guilt inside me. My defense mechanism was to be an asshole. We'd argue, say hurtful things neither of us could take back, and then we wouldn't talk for months. It was our routine, and one I didn't see changing anytime soon.

"Would you like some more water, sir?" The waitress asked for the third time.

I handed her my glass, and she refilled it before handing it back. She picked up the empty dinner plate in front of me and set the check face-down on the table. "I'll take this whenever you're ready."

"Thanks." I took a long draw of my water, the icy coldness of it almost burning my throat as it descended to settle in my stomach. I smirked at the imaginary sloshing sound it probably made hitting the inside of my gut. My humor always leaned toward the dark side.

My gaze traveled around the room, my leg bouncing in a nervous twitch. The hotel restaurant was slow tonight. Which was surprising for a weekend. A lot of empty tables, and only three people sitting at the bar—four, if I counted the suit-clad businessman, with his smarmy salesman smile looming over a blonde woman. My bobbing limb slowed. Old boy certainly wasn't taking the hint that blondie wasn't interested. In fact, she was as oblivious to his presence as he seemed to be to the fact she was practically collapsing in on herself. He ran his finger down her arm, and she shifted on the bar stool, putting a few inches of distance between them.

I'd never been the savior type. Fuck, I couldn't even save myself. But there was a tightness to her, a rigid energy, that screamed for help. Before I changed my mind, I rose from the corner booth I'd parked myself at and strode toward the couple. I should mind my own business. If the woman wanted the guy to leave she could tell him. But for whatever reason, my feet kept propelling me forward until I stood on the woman's right, close enough she could hear me speak, but far enough away that I didn't invade her personal space. Unlike dickwad.

"Is this guy bothering you?" I asked softly.

The woman flinched and the suit straightened and sent me a withering look, like I was a pile of shit he'd stepped in with his favorite wingtip shoes.

"Who the fuck are you?" He sneered.

I ignored him. Instead, I waited for the woman to answer. Her response was the only one I gave a shit about.

She continued staring down into her almost empty rocks glass, her wavy blonde hair a curtain over the side of her face.

"I just want to be left alone." There was a note of emotion in her tone. One I'd heard more than once in rehab and during the many NA meetings I'd attended over the years from those who'd hit rock bottom. It was the bitter tone of anguish.

I smirked at the suit. "Pretty sure that's your cue. The lady's not interested."

He glared at me before sending her a scathing look and

picked up the drink he'd set on the bar. "Whatever." Then he disappeared with a final curl of his lip.

Not once during the entire interaction had she glanced up at either of us. She'd stayed hidden behind the armor of her hair. Aside from her single sentence to be left alone, she hadn't spoken again. Not even a thank you. Taking her at her word, my presence was also not wanted or needed. I returned to my booth and took another drink, my eyes continuing to dart back to the blonde every so often.

The bartender brought her several more drinks. She sipped each one, her delicate fingers clasping the glass, condensation dripping off the bottom of it. After suit guy left, no one else bothered her. She sat alone, completely lost in her own world. Yet I remained sitting here, watching the woman like some creeper.

There was something about her that kept nudging at me. Some compulsion kept me here. I'd only seen a portion of her face through the cascade of her hair. Her cheekbones appeared sharp enough to cut glass. A pale pink lip-color did nothing to plump up her too thin lips. The tip of her nose curved upward. None of the pieces fit together.

It was her eyes, though, that I hadn't caught a glimpse of.

I'd moved to stand near her, spoke to her, smelled her—a hint of lavender and vanilla—and still she'd remained gazing into her glass as though it held some secret. What was her story?

After a quick glance at my watch, I was shocked that it was nearly nine p.m. *Jesus, how had it gotten so late?* I'd been observing her for over two hours. A time in which my earlier urge had quieted. She'd occupied my entire mind, so it hadn't focused on anything but her. I was reluctant to leave, but I needed to go. I dug out my wallet and threw enough cash on the table to pay the bill plus a tip.

The woman had made it clear she wanted to be left alone, but I wanted to check one last time to make sure she was all right before I headed out. Especially after watching her slam back the rest of yet another drink. A pull from some string drew me over to her.

"Excuse me." I waited a beat to see if she'd finally look at me. She didn't, but I forged ahead. "I'm not trying to bother you, but I wanted to make sure you were okay before I left."

Behind the fall of her hair, her lids drifted shut for a moment before they opened again. She slowly raised her head and stared directly in front of her. No other movement. I took the silence as her answer.

"I hear ya loud and clear. Just…be careful." I pivoted, but her whispered request stopped me in my tracks.

"Don't go."

SUBMISSION

"YOU CAN DO THIS," I muttered to myself while I peeped out my car windshield. With a deep exhale, I wiped my sweaty palms on my pant leg and tried to calm the butterflies in my belly. I could feel my heart beating in my ears. I'd been sitting here for thirty minutes. I looked down at the ridiculous container of store-bought potato salad. It was probably getting warm. And gross.

I caught movement out of my periphery. Just a couple walking to their car. I didn't know what I hoped to see from my parking space way in the back. The longer I sat there, though, the greater the urge was to leave. But damn it, I'd come this far. What could it hurt to mingle a little? I mean, these were just normal people, right? Kinky people, but still totally normal. Except for me. I was as vanilla as they came. Or was I? That's what I was here to find out.

Now or never. With that, I quickly grabbed the stupid plastic tub and exited my car before I changed my mind. With a determined stride, I made my way across the parking lot and up the sidewalk toward the shelter house. My steps stuttered briefly when heads turned at my entrance. I gave an awkward smile and set my offering in an empty space between a tin pan of burnt hot dogs and a mostly empty baking dish of what looked like macaroni and cheese.

When I turned back around, no one was paying me any attention. Trying to remain inconspicuous, I stepped off to the side to stand against the wall, observing those sitting at the picnic tables scattered around.

"Well, who do we have here?" A deep, gravelly voice at my right drew my attention. My breath hitched and my body heated when I spotted the sexiest man I'd ever laid eyes on. I'd always been a sucker for a man with salt and pepper hair. Damn, he filled out that navy t-shirt nicely. My eyes traveled his full length before returning to his face. I flushed at the amused half-smile he wore at my perusal. It took me a moment to remember he'd asked me a question.

"Pe-Penny," I stuttered, almost breathless as the heat in my face intensified. I don't remember blushing this much before in my life. *Fake it 'til you make it* was my mantra. I stood a little taller and attempted to gain the confidence I typically displayed with chauvinistic surgeons.

"I'm Marcus." His secret smile remained as he reached out to shake my hand. When I placed mine in his, he squeezed it firmly, and I thought I felt his thumb gently caress mine, but he pulled away before I could be sure.

"Nice to meet you." The words came out a little shaky.

"So, what brings you out to play with us today?" His voice dropped suggestively.

Maintaining my barely-there confidence, I answered his question. "I'm curious about domination and submission. I figured this was the best place to gain some knowledge."

"Knowledge about what?" Marcus asked, showing true interest.

Everything. I wanted to know what it felt like to give up control.

To just feel and not have to think.

To be dominated.

To have someone fulfill needs I didn't even know I had.

I wanted to find my happily ever after, damn it. Sadly, I didn't know how to express any of this.

I shrugged my shoulders. "Whatever someone will teach me."

"Sweetness," he murmured, "I'd be happy to teach you anything you want to know. In the meantime, why don't I introduce you to some friends of mine."

With a hand across my lower back, startling me with the sparks of electricity that flowed through my extremities, Marcus led me over to a group of women.

"Ladies, I'd like to introduce you to Penny. This is her first munch. She's here getting the lay of the land, so to speak. I have no doubt you'll make her feel welcome." There was an undercurrent of command in his tone.

I sat on the bench and Marcus moved away. The back of my neck tingled like I was still being watched, but I ignored the sensation.

"Hi, I'm Bridget."

My eyes landed on a gorgeous redhead with chocolate-colored eyes and a bright, welcoming smile that seemed genuine. She looked about my age. She continued introducing the rest of the group while she pointed at each woman who waved when she spoke their name. "That's Delilah, Jackie, and Priscilla, but we call her Priss."

"Nice to meet you."

"Soooo," she drew out the word, "I assume you're a sub?"

"Um, I'm not really sure."

She laughed. "Well, if you're not, then Marcus there is going to be sadly disappointed."

My face heated.

"He hasn't taken his eyes off you since the moment you sat down." This came from Delilah.

"I'm sure he's just making sure everyone is having a good time." I tried brushing off their words.

They all continued to stare at me in a placating way.

Bridget spoke up. "If you say so."

I quickly changed the topic. "So, are there munches held very often?"

Thankfully, they let the previous topic go. "We have a munch at The Local Cue on the first Friday of every month."

"The Local Cue?" I asked Priss, I think her name was.

"It's a billiards club over on Hamilton Street."

Bridget chimed in. "You should totally come next week."

We continued talking for the next hour or so. I learned so much listening to them talk about their lifestyle. It was fascinating. Soon though, the potluck was winding down, and I needed to get going.

"Thank you all for making me feel welcome. I debating getting out of my car for over thirty minutes, and I'm so glad I did. This was fun. I'm definitely going to come on Friday."

Bridget stood when I did, and I was surprised when she pulled me into a hug.

"It was so nice to meet you. I really do hope you'll come this weekend. We have so much fun and there are a ton of people I can introduce you to. We're an open and accepting group. Let me give you my phone number. If you ever have any questions about anything or just want someone to talk to, give me a call."

We exchanged phone numbers and I waved goodbye to everyone. I hadn't made it five feet before a sinful voice stopped me.

"Have you discovered any deep, dark secrets yet?" Marcus asked.

"Yours or mine?" I slowly turned to face him.

Marcus stepped closer and closer, edging me backward until I was flush with the wall behind me. The wall where this day began. He stopped just short of touching me. Instead, he leaned down, his warm breath caressing my ear.

"Why, yours, of course. I'm curious to know what depraved secrets you keep buried that you wish someone like me would discover. In fact, I think I would enjoy that immensely. Discovering your secrets, that is. Secrets I'm going to bet involve all the scandalous things you've fanta-sized about. A man binding your hands above your head while he feasts on your your sweet, succulent cunt."

I whimpered at the picture he painted, and my knees almost gave out. He was right. I did have those fantasies. I had to brace myself against the cement at my back.

He continued when he sensed my arousal. "You want to be fucked harder than you've ever been fucked before. Your ass spanked. You want to come like you've never come before."

Every scene flashed through my mind and god did I want it. I wanted everything he described. It terrified me this ecstasy flowing through me. I didn't even know this man, but I had a feeling that if, given the chance, he'd discover all my secrets.

Overwhelmed by the onslaught, I gasped. "I have to go."

Start the best-selling series today with SUBMISSION.
FREE with Kindle Unlimited!
Amazon: https://amzn.to/2WeWvHv

ACKNOWLEDGMENTS

This is the part where I struggle to make sure I don't forget every person who helped make this book possible. You would think I'd learn by now to start keeping a list as I go. Sigh. I know I'm going to forget someone, and I'll feel like an asshole even though they'll never mention it. I'm going to do my best!

Thank you to my amazing author friends who constantly listen to me bitch, moan, and whine. Julia Sykes and Autumn Jones Lake, you two are my bad ass bitches. Thank you both for everything!

Thank you to my fantastic editor, Dayna Hart. You deal with my constant inability to hit a deadline and your insight and suggestions always make me think.

Thank you to my writing coach, Lauren Clarke, at Creating Ink. You've taught me so much about craft over these last few months. I think Striking Distance is so much better for it.

Thank you to my alpha readers, Kathryn Parson and Antje Cartaxo. Your thoughtful comments, critiques, and suggestions made Striking Distance better!

Thank you to L. Woods PR and my publicist, Nicole Jackson, for all your hard work. I appreciate you.

Thank you to all the bloggers and bookstagrammers who shared Striking Distance with their readers! I appreciate all the hard work you guys do to run your blogs and pages.

Thank you to all the readers I've met both online and in person. I'm so thankful for all your support over the years. Thank you for loving my stories and sharing them with your friends. You are all absolutely amazing, and I couldn't do this without you!

Much love,
LK

Doms of Club Eden

Submission

Desire

Redemption

Protect

Betrayal

My Christmas Dom

Absolution

Forever (A prequel) - Coming July 2020

Love Undercover Series

In Too Deep

Striking Distance

Atonement

Other Books

Love Notes: A Dark Romance

SEALs in Love

Say Yes

Black Light: Possession

Saving Evie: A Brotherhood Protectors

LK Shaw resides in South Carolina with her high maintenance beagle mix dog, Miss P. An avid reader since childhood, she became hooked on historical romance novels in high school. She now reads, and loves, all romance sub-genres, with dark romance and romantic suspense being her favorite. LK enjoys traveling and chocolate. Her books feature hot alpha heroes and the strong women they love.

Want a FREE short story? Be sure to sign up for my newsletter and download your copy of A Birthday Spanking, a Doms of Club Eden prequel!
http://bit.ly/LKShawNewsletter

LK loves to interact with readers. You can follow her on any of her social media:

LK Shaw's Club Eden: https://www.facebook.com/groups/LKShawsClubEden
Author Page: www.facebook.com/LKShawAuthor
Author Profile: www.facebook.com/AuthorLKShaw
IG: @LKShaw_Author
Amazon: www.amazon.com/author/lkshaw
Bookbub: https://www.bookbub.com/authors/lk-shaw
Website: www.lkshawauthor.com